the sorta sisters

Ω

Published by
PEACHTREE PUBLISHERS
1700 Chattahoochee Avenue
Atlanta, Georgia 30318-2112
www.peachtree-online.com

Book and cover design by Adrian Fogelin and Loraine M. Joyner

Printed in the United States of America
10 9 8 7 6 5 4 3 2 1
First Edition

Library of Congress Cataloging-in-Publication Data

Fogelin, Adrian.
  The sorta sisters / by Adrian Fogelin. -- 1st ed.
    p. cm.
  Summary: In Florida, Anna Casey lives with what she hopes is the last in a long line of foster mothers, and Mica Delano lives with her father on their small boat, and when the two of them begin corresponding, they discover they have a lot in common.
  ISBN 13: 978-1-56145-424-2
  ISBN 10: 1-56145-424-9
  [1. Friendship--Fiction. 2. Foster home care--Fiction. 3. Single parent families--Fiction. 4. Alcoholism--Fiction. 5. Letters--Fiction. 6. Florida--Fiction.] I. Title.
  PZ7.F72635So 2007
  [Fic]--dc22
                                     2007011735

the sorta

sisters

Adrian Fogelin

Ω
PEACHTREE
ATLANTA

For Margaret, Vicky, Barbara, Kathy, Loraine, Laura, Melanie,
Queen Maureen, the double K twins, Mimi, Amy,
and all my Sorta Sisters at Peachtree Publishers

Thanks to my dear friends,
The Wednesday Night Writers:
Richard Dempsey, Gina Edwards, Leigh Muller,
Noanne Gwynn, and Linda Sturgeon

And a big thanks to my dad, Carl Fogelin,
who paid my way through art school—
See, I *did* learn a thing or two!

chapter 1

"HEY, GIRL, WANT TO TAKE a look?" Anna knows that no dog—not even an exceptional one like Beauty—is interested in the night sky. It's just that the moon through her new telescope is too big and too awesome to keep to herself. She wants to share it.

Beauty rolls onto her back at Anna's feet and grins up at her. The dog's teeth glow in the pale light of the streetlamp, and so do the white patches on her splotchy coat. Anna drops to one knee. "Would the exceptional dog like a belly rub?"

As she scratches the dog's stomach, a chilly gust cuts through her old sweater. "It's cold, isn't it, girl?" She works her fingers through Beauty's thick fur until she can feel the radiating dog warmth.

The streetlamp three houses away paints the road with twisted shadows; the shadow of the telescope is a giant spider. When Anna stands, her shadow-legs are long and stalky, her shadow-head a mere bump. She lifts the hat she always wears. The misshapen shadow-girl lifts her hat too.

As she pulls on her uncle's old hat, the wind slaps the brim back. She wraps her arms around herself and leans into the telescope, pressing an eye to the eyepiece.

"What if the moon were only as big as it looks through the 'scope? I'd reach up and grab it for my collection."

Anna's collection contains one rock for each place she's lived over the last ten years—so many rocks that they barely fit on the windowsill in her new room. She hugs herself harder. "The moon would be a great last rock."

Miss Johnette, her latest foster mom, is going to become her real mom. "Hopefully," Anna whispers, resting a hand on the barrel of the telescope. "This telescope is too expensive to give to a kid you don't plan to keep."

She stares at the lit windows of Miss J's house. Stuccoed in white with a cheerful purple door, all it needs is snow on the roof to look like a cottage on a Christmas card.

Snow will never fall here—this *is* Florida. But Anna wishes that everything could stay the same as it is right now, like a Christmas card. Miss J says it will, but Anna's lived with scads of aunts and uncles and cousins, in forever places that didn't last. Even though they were her family, it never worked out. In the end, she was always one too many.

Miss Johnette is not a member of Anna's real family. Anyone can tell they aren't related. Miss J is tall and big boned; Anna is small. Miss J calls the two of them "a family by choice." Anna loves Miss J and trusts her, but until she is legally and officially adopted, anything can happen.

"It's New Year's Day," she tells the dog. "The very first day of our best year ever." She doesn't know if there is such a thing as a New Year's wish, but she makes one just in case, crossing her fingers to help it come true.

She has just pressed her eye back against the eyepiece when she hears the *click...click...click* of bike gears, then the scrape of a sneaker on the road. "What're you doing?" asks a boy voice.

She turns and—*ohmygosh!* It's Ben Floyd, back from his family vacation in the Keys. "Observing the full moon," she says.

She's thought about Ben all Christmas break. But now, sitting there breathing through his mouth, bike angled awkwardly between his legs, he's not as cute as he was in her daydreams— until he flicks his head to get his hair out of his eyes.

She feels her face flush. To give herself something to do, she shifts the legs of the tripod a few inches. "I got this great telescope for Christmas. Want to see?" She steps back and twists her hands down to the bottom of her pockets.

For a moment he just rests his weight on stiff arms, his hands on the handlebars. Then, with a slower *click…click…click,* he wheels over. "It won't be full until tomorrow night," he says, ducking his head to take a look.

"True." If he knows that, he must be interested in the moon too. That's something they have in common.

But he can't be *that* interested because he doesn't look for long. "Nice 'scope." The way he says it sounds like good-bye. He turns the front wheel, puts a foot on the pedal, then stops and pats the pocket of his denim jacket. "Hey, Anna, I have a letter for you." He slides a small, lumpy bundle out of his pocket.

"You do?" Her heart rises. "Who from?" *Him—it has to be from him!*

"A girl who was staying at the marina. She lives aboard a sailboat and travels around with her dad."

Anna feels her heart fall like an egg out of a nest and land with a splat.

He doesn't notice that she's not listening. "She goes to school by mail. Her name is Mica."

He seems to be waiting for her to say something, so she parrots back the last thing she heard him say. "She lives on a boat? Cool."

"Now don't go squeezing it," he warns as he sets the package in her hand. "There's a fragile shell inside. A janthina. Tell you more about it later. I gotta go." He pulls something flat out of the back pocket of his jeans and moves it carefully to his shirt pocket.

It's probably a letter for someone else—one he wrote himself. Maybe the pendant Cass Bodine wears around her neck really is a Christmas present from him, Anna thinks. *Everyone says it is.*

Holding the small bundle to her chest, Anna watches him pedal away. "Where are you going?" she shouts.

"Gotta see somebody," he yells over his shoulder. He stands on the pedals, picking up speed.

"Thanks for the letter," she calls after him. "And the shell. Say hi to Cass." If he's on his way to see Justin or Leroy, he'll circle back to set her straight, but he doesn't.

It must be true about the necklace.

Imagining that he could have liked me was stupid, Anna thinks now. Besides, Cass is nice. Anna tries to be happy for her.

She puts her eye to the eyepiece, but all she sees is half a moon—which is all he saw too. The other half was lost when she moved the telescope. He didn't say a thing, or adjust the angle. Guess he doesn't care about the moon after all.

If she stays outside he'll go by again on his way home, but it doesn't matter. He isn't any closer than the moon, not really.

Johnette Walker quits whistling when she hears the front door open. She glances up from the fossils she's sorting on the kitchen table. "Anna?" Beauty, a streak with brown and white spots, scrambles into the kitchen and slides across the linoleum, then flops down in front of the wood stove.

"Just a sec," Anna calls from the living room. "I have to make a phone call."

Good, Johnette thinks, leaning over to pat the dog. *She's calling someone from school.* Maybe it's her imagination, but Anna seems a little light on friends. In the next room Anna asks for Cass, but seconds later Anna walks into the kitchen, shoulders slumped. Johnette wonders what's wrong, but doesn't know how to ask. "Hey, I was about to join you outside."

"It's kind of cold."

Anna is wearing that thin sweater again, the hand-me-down from her cousin with the buttons that dangle by loose threads. Johnette wonders if wearing the sweater with the iron-on label that says "Janice Casey" is more important to Anna than staying warm. She has so few things from her family.

But what if Anna catches a cold? How do *real* mothers know what is important and what they can let slide? Johnette reaches out and runs a hand down one thin sweater sleeve. "Were you warm enough?"

Anna shrugs.

That means no. Johnette remembers that much from being a kid herself. She puts the sweater on her things-to-fix-later list. "What's that?" she asks, pointing at the small bundle in Anna's hand.

The girl holds out a crumpled sheet of lined notebook paper tied with a piece of yarn. "Ben gave it to me." She blushes when she says his name.

When Johnette was Anna's age she was too busy tramping around collecting bugs to be interested in boys. But Anna seems interested. The question is, is it time for boys to be interested back? Johnette hopes not. She's having a hard enough time figuring out what to do about the sweater. "Ben wrote you a note?"

"No." Anna tucks her hair behind her ear, acting as if it doesn't matter. "Ben likes Cass."

"Then who wrote you?"

"A girl Ben met on vacation. She lives on a boat." Anna sits down opposite her and balances the packet on her outstretched hand. "There's supposed to be a shell in it, but it feels way too light."

Johnette scoots the kitchen chair forward. "Let's have a little look-see."

Carefully, carefully, Anna folds back the paper. When she concentrates, even her freckles seem to pay attention.

Anna smooths the crumpled paper against the table, exposing the lavender shell inside. "It's as thin as paper and as beautiful as the moon," she says, almost whispering. Miss J feels her heart squeeze. Do all kids say things like that, or just hers? Their social worker, Mrs. Riley, says that every child is special—and that every child has limitations.

Every child but my Anna, thinks Johnette, propping her chin on one hand. *My Anna is perfect.* "Well? What does the girl on the boat have to say?"

Anna picks up the letter and begins to read.

January 1 (Happy New Year!)
Dear Anna Casey,

Hi. My name is Mica (like the rock) Delano. I know
your friend Ben and his little brother Cody. Their aunt and
uncle (I call them Aunt Emma and Uncle Bert too) own the
marina where my father and I dock our sailboat. I spent
Christmas with the guys.

Are you <u>really</u> reading this??? If you are it means Ben
actually delivered it. I bet he told you about me. <u>Forget
everything he said.</u> This is the real truth. I'm eleven. Skinny
but cute. Better than him when it comes to fishing, diving,
snorkeling, swimming, etc., etc., etc. My dad and I live
aboard a 32-foot sailboat called the Martina. I go to school
by mail. I'm on the ninth-grade level.

Ben told me all about you. I think we're a lot alike (see list):
1. We both like science.
2. We move around a lot—you as a foster kid and me
because I live on a boat.
3. We each live with one parent. I have the Captain (that's
what I call my dad). You have your foster mom.

Did the shell make it okay? It's a janthina. The Latin name
is <u>Janthina janthina.</u> Ben told me your foster mom teaches
biology. The Captain says that makes her almost a biologist,

so she might know about Latin names. She's probably heard of my dad. He's the world-famous marine biologist Dr. Robin Michael Delano.

More stuff about the shell: The janthina snail hangs upside down below the surface of the water. It floats because it's attached to a raft of bubbles that gets pushed by the wind and current. Janthinas wash up on the beach a lot. A janthina doesn't get to choose where it goes.

Our sailboat is like a janthina. She rides the wind and currents, but we decide where she goes—at least the Captain does.

Questions (please answer):
1. What is your favorite animal? Mine is a bottlenose dolphin, <u>Tursiops truncates</u> (Latin again).
2. Don't you think dolphins look sympathetic? The Captain says animals don't have emotions, but sometimes they swim alongside the <u>Martina</u> and look at me with one little eye and smile like they're keeping me company. Aunt Emma took me to Theater of the Sea to swim with dolphins. We didn't tell the Captain. He doesn't approve of wild animals being used for entertainment.
3. What is the scariest thing that ever happened to you? One time we got caught in a squall and the mast snapped.

The Captain made me go below. I didn't know for a long time if he was still up there or if he had washed overboard. Then there was the time I fell in quicksand.

4. Have you ever seen snow? I haven't, but plan to as soon as possible.

5. Do you have any brothers or sisters? (I have zero.)

This letter is getting really long, which is stupid. If Ben didn't give it to you, he's probably reading it himself. If you are, Spaz Boy, you are soooooooo dead!

If it is Anna who is reading this, please write back sooooooooooooooon. The Captain could decide to sail at any time!

Send your reply to: Mica Delano, c/o Bert's Marina, P.O. Box 645, Islamorada, FL 33036.

> Your friend in science,
> Mica Delano

P.S. It would be way faster to e-mail but the Captain only lets me use his computer for homework, and only when he's right there—no privacy. Plus it's hard to e-mail a shell.

chapter 2

WAVELETS RISE AND FALL against Mica's cheeks as she floats on her back in the canal in front of Bert's Marina. The flag snaps over the nearby Coast Guard station; the sea must be choppy today. But her canal, which pokes off Snake Creek like a thumb, is protected from the wind.

She likes Bert's Marina. Likes it a lot. If it were up to her she'd stay forever. But when the Captain's short job at Biology Fun Camp ends—which will be soon, since the holidays are over and the camp is down to a trickle of school groups—they'll leave. She just *has* to hear back from Anna Casey before then. What if the letter comes the day after they leave? Even one minute after they cast off would be too late! The letter would be sitting in the box at the Islamorada post office when the *Martina* left the slip. She and the Captain would be unfurling the *Martina*'s sails when Aunt Emma picked it up. Too bad. Return to sender.

If Anna had written back immediately it would be here already; maybe it got lost. Or maybe she isn't going to write at all. Because maybe Ben never delivered the letter. But it is just possible that Anna's reply is in the post office box right now. *I wouldn't know, though,* Mica says to herself. *Aunt Emma won't leave even for a few teeny minutes to take me to the post office.* Aunt Emma is waiting for a call from Chicago where her latest grand-baby is getting itself born.

But that shouldn't keep them from going to the post office. Uncle Bert can answer the phone. And if the baby gets born while they're away, so what? It'll *still* be born when they get back.

Mica has pointed all those things out to Aunt Emma. She's begged and begged. (Even if you can't convince adults, you can sometimes wear them down.) She'd try again now, but her last beg was only ten minutes ago.

She takes a deep breath and holds it. Her skinny chest rises out of the water. Suddenly she has a shivery thought: *This is the way dead people look when they float.* She lets her arms and legs go limp and pretends she's dead—it's not like she has anything better to do.

She's still lying there lifeless when she hears the buzz of a small engine. She lifts her head just long enough to see the Captain's moped hurtle into the marina parking lot. He squeals to a stop and cuts the engine.

Ka-thunkita-thunkita-thunkita. The wheels of the moped make a tired sound against the boards of the dock. With thin, strong arms her father pushes the bike past the pair of rusty gas pumps where boaters fuel up and past the *Lizzy-J,* a twenty-four-foot powerboat waiting for Uncle Bert to replace a bent prop. She watches him through squinted eyes, expecting that at any moment he'll see her floating in the boat basin—dead!

He still hasn't seen her when he and the moped disappear behind Aunt Emma and Uncle Bert's houseboat.

When her father reappears, his eyes are on the water but he's facing away from her, peering into the shallows between the dock and dry land. He cocks his head so he can see through the reflections.

"Yes!" he exclaims. He drops the moped against a piling and snatches the net that lies on the picnic table near their boat. With the net he dips up a knot of seaweed, which he dumps into one of the bubbling aquariums on the table. Resting his weight on his arms, he gazes at what she knows must be the fish that was hiding in the seaweed.

Darn it! She *knew* he needed a sargassum fish to illustrate protective coloration. She's been trying to find one for him for days. But it isn't easy. The fish are blotched and splotched with white, yellow, and gray, just like the seaweed they hide in.

Her father can see anything in the water.

Except her.

And she's not even camouflaged. The water is blue. She's tanned a dark brown. Her swimsuit is printed with hot pink hibiscus and bright macaws. How could he miss her?

Through half-closed eyelids, she watches him turn and gaze out over the basin.

Now! He'll see her now! She lets her tongue hang out a little.

He shades his eyes—and studies the flag on the Coast Guard station. He's judging the wind speed and direction, which he'll record in his weather journal. He lifts the pith helmet he always wears and lets the wind blow through his thin brown hair. His wide-legged khaki shorts flutter in the breeze. Still not seeing her, he hobbles over to the *Martina* and pulls himself up onto the deck, his arms doing most of the work. The hatch scrapes and he disappears below.

Mica whips her head out of the water. "Hel-lo! I'm dead down here!"

The only answer is the closing of the hatch.

She tells herself there are plenty of reasons he didn't see her. He's been teaching kids all day. Except for her, he hates kids. He only took the job because neither of the grants he's applied for has come through yet. And she can tell by his limp that his bad leg aches.

But by not noticing her, isn't he breaking his promise? One week ago when Ben and Cody were still here, the three of them got lost at sea. It scared the Captain so bad he swore that he would stay home more and pay better attention to her.

If he's so busy paying attention, why didn't her see her? He saw an invisible fish, didn't he?

Suddenly his promise seems hollow, like a New Year's resolution. She doesn't want to think about it. It must be time to bug Aunt Emma again.

How did I get talked into this? Emma thinks as she pulls the van into the post office parking lot. *What if the phone is ringing right this very minute? Bert said he'll get it, but he won't.*

She and Mica have just climbed out of the van when Emma spots Wiley Millman's golden retriever with his head out the window of Wiley's pickup. This is all she needs! Mica will have to stop and give old Jethro a pat. Emma slows, accepting the inevitable, but the girl walks right past. "Mica, aren't you going to pat Jethro?"

"Maybe on the way out," Mica calls over her shoulder.

Good—the dog might be gone by then. Emma wouldn't have mentioned it, but Mica needs all the affection she can get, even if it's just a friendly slobber.

Mica and her father often rent dock space at the marina for their live-aboard sailboat. They usually stay a month or two before moving on. Emma has never gotten the straight story about Mica's mother—Mica has described her as everything from a famous ballet dancer to a CIA spy. The only thing Emma knows for sure is that in all the times the father and daughter have tied up at the marina, she's never once laid eyes on the woman.

Emma allows the girl to call her *Aunt* Emma because it gives Mica a little more family. But it's hardly enough. The child is alone far too much. Homeschooled, she rarely has other kids to play with. Emma lets Mica do her studying perched on the spare stool in the marina office. And she showed her how to help around the store, pumping gas and dipping bait shrimp from the tank, just to keep her busy.

If the girl were here for any significant length of time, Emma would insist she be enrolled in public school. Sometimes Mica just wears her out. Today she begged and begged to go to the post office, until Emma finally gave in.

"What's the rush?" Emma asks as Mica streaks ahead up the walk to the post office. "Are you expecting something?"

The scrawny girl holds the door open. "Come *on*."

That's when Emma figures it out. Ever since her husband's nephew brought his family down over Christmas, Mica has badgered her to go to the post office. *Of course. Mica is waiting for a letter from Ben.*

Trailing Mica to the post office box, she tries to see Ben the way an eleven-year-old girl would. He's tall and lanky with dark hair, dark eyes. Cute—and a good kid too. But that doesn't mean he'll send her a letter. "Boys aren't reliable letter writers…" she warns gently.

"Boys? What boys?"

This girl is good at hiding things, but the innocent look doesn't fool Emma.

By the time Emma reaches box 645, Mica has her eyes up to the little glass pane in the brass door. "Stuffed!" she announces.

"With the usual junk, I'm sure." Emma unlocks the box and wiggles out the envelopes and fliers.

On most post office visits Mica wanders around staring at posters of criminals. Traveling as much as she does, she says that it is "more than possible" that one day she'll recognize one of the faces and collect a big reward. But today she follows Emma to the narrow table by the window.

"Boys are the worst letter writers," Emma warns.

"Who said anything about boys?" Poised on her bare toes, Mica watches Emma sort the mail into two piles: "keepers" and "tossers."

"The absolute worst letter writers…and I bet Ben is no different."

"Ben!" Mica huffs. "Why would I want a letter from Spaz Boy?" But she brushes aside the long bangs she often hides behind so she can have an unobstructed view of the mail.

"Nothing special," Emma announces as the stack of mail dwindles. If she could shake a letter out of her great nephew, Emma would do it just to see this girl smile. Ben probably hadn't even noticed Mica—not like that. At thirteen and a half, Ben has to see an eleven-year-old as a baby.

But the last piece of mail isn't a flier from Sears or an ad from Evinrude or the latest *Reader's Digest*. It's a bulky white envelope addressed in ballpoint pen.

"Mica, honey? You got a letter!"

Mica snatches the envelope out of her hand and spins on her toes. "Look," she says, holding it out to Aunt Emma. "Thick! Thick! Thick!"

Aunt Emma squints at the return address, then lowers the reading glasses that, as usual, rest on the top of her head.

"Tallahassee! You don't suppose that nephew of mine… No, it's from someone named A. Casey. Do you know someone named A. Casey in Tallahassee?"

"Definitely." For a moment the girl holds the letter to her chest. "Well, sort of." Her shaggy brown hair falls in front of her eyes as she sniffs the envelope.

"Does it have a smell?"

"Just plain old paper." Mica pushes her bangs out of her eyes and grins. "Good. That means she isn't all girlie."

"There's nothing wrong with being a *little* bit girlie." Sometimes Emma just itches to give Mica's knotty hair a good brushing or buy her something nice to wear. She's being raised by a man and it shows.

Mica plunks the letter on the postal scale. "One point eight ounces!"

"That's a lot of words…" Emma picks up the letter and gives it a squeeze. Something squishy is folded up inside. "Aren't you going to open it?" she asks, handing it to Mica.

"Later."

The breeze through the van window blows Mica's mane of hair across her face all the way back to the marina, but she uses both hands to hold on to the envelope in her lap. Emma assumes that she wants to be alone when she reads it, but when Emma comes back into the office from checking with Bert—no, the baby isn't born yet—Mica is sitting on her usual stool, the letter on the sales counter in front of her.

Emma settles on the stool across from her. They both stare at the envelope.

"Is it later yet?" Emma asks. "Because if it isn't, I'll just die of curiosity."

"Later enough." The girl swoops up the letter and jams a finger under the envelope flap, but then she stops. She tears it open slowly, carefully—and Emma realizes that never, in all the on-and-off times Mica and her father have docked at Bert's Marina, has Mica ever received a letter, not even from her secret agent ballerina mother.

Mica holds her breath as she slides out the yellow lined pages. "Let's see what the lump in the middle is."

Mica unfolds the paper, revealing a split and withered seed-pod. Just then a light breeze blows through the open office door. The seeds, each attached to a silky parachute, stir as if waking up. They billow across the room. Some land on the shelves of motor oil, some on the rope display. One catches in the petals of a rose made entirely of tarpon scales; a woman in Emma's church makes them for the tourists. A few seeds float the length of the shop and drift out the door into the bay where Bert is repairing an engine.

"They look like tiny angels," Emma says.

"Angels aren't real."

"Oh, they're real," Aunt Emma says softly. "Science just doesn't know about them."

They might as well be angels the way Mica watches them float across the room. The last seed is near the open door when Mica jumps off her stool and catches it. She stuffs the bit of fluff in the pocket of her shorts.

"What does the girl in Tallahassee have to say?"

Mica unfolds the letter. "Hey, look, there's a picture of a butterfly in here too!" She hands Emma the photo, then smooths the letter against the glass countertop and starts to read.

Dear Mica,

We <u>are</u> alike, except you move around on water and I move around on land—only not anymore I hope. Miss Johnette (my foster mom) and I are really really happy together, so maybe this is my last home—at least until college, if I go.

Thanks for the shell. Miracle! Ben didn't sit on it. I put it on the windowsill with my rock collection (one rock from each place I've lived). My collection is complete now, I hope, which means I have room for extras like shells.

The pod inside this letter is from a milkweed. Most of them froze a couple of weeks ago (no snow here in Tallahassee, but sometimes frost). This one was near the house so it was okay. Milkweed seeds are like janthinas. They don't get to choose where they go either. The wind just takes them. But once a seed lands, it puts down a root so deep you can never pull it up.

Miss J grows lots of milkweeds. Their leaves are the favorite food of monarch butterfly caterpillars (<u>Danaus plexippus</u>—we don't mind Latin either). Most gardeners poison or squish caterpillars. But Miss J says that if you want butterflies you have to feed caterpillars—that's the deal.

Last fall we tagged migrating monarchs. They fly through here on their way to Mexico (or wherever???). We're tagging them to find out for sure where they go. A few of our tagged butterflies have been found in Mexico—not many though. We think some of them are going south down the peninsula of Florida—maybe even to the Keys. Keep your eyes open for orange and black butterflies with stickers on their wings (see picture).

Miss J thought the part about her almost being a "real biologist" was pretty funny. She says to remind the Captain that biology teachers inspire kids to become biologists—which is almost like reproduction, and there's nothing more biological than reproduction. Gross!!!!!!!!

She hasn't heard of the Captain, but don't feel bad. Most of the biologists she knows about are dead.

Answers:

1. My favorite animal is my dog Beauty (<u>Canis familiaris</u>). I got her at the animal shelter. She was hit by a car before I adopted her. She's missing a few minor parts but she's still the best. I think the Captain is wrong. <u>All</u> animals have emotions. Beauty gets happy, sad, excited, calm. She smiles like a dolphin and talks with her tail and her ear. (She only has one, but it is very expressive.)

2. The scariest thing that ever happened to me was when my grandmother died. I lived with her after my parents died. (Which was scary too, I guess—I was only two so I don't remember.)

After Grandma died I got passed around my family. Then I got put in foster care (also scary)—which is where I met Miss J. We'll be family forever, I hope.

3. I saw plenty of snow when I lived up north. There are basically two kinds. Wet and dry. Wet makes good snowballs. Dry is better if you want to look at the crystals. After it's been on the ground a couple of days it gets dirty, but at first it's beautiful.

4. No, I don't have any brothers or sisters. Since you don't either, maybe we could be honorary sisters.

My questions for you:

1. Where do you sleep? A hammock or a bed?

2. Do you ever get lonely going to school by yourself? Regular school can be lonely too. Especially when you switch schools a lot.

3. Do you think Ben Floyd is cute? Everyone here falls all over him. His girlfriend Cass is nice.

4. Did your mom die? You don't have to say if you don't want to. But since mine did, I know how that feels.

Your (sorta) sister,
Anna

chapter 3

MICA FLOATS. THE PENNY she's been tossing and diving after rests on the chest of her bright swimsuit. Overhead a Magnificent Frigate Bird with wiry wings wheels across the sky like a lazy scribble.

She sings the bird's secret Latin name softly, "*Fregata magnificens*," then louder, "*Fre-gaaa-taaa mag-ni-fi-cens!*" Mica feels for the penny and picks it up. She lifts her arm out of the water and flings the coin as hard as she can. It sails up and out. It flickers against the sky, then lands with a satisfying *plunk* in the middle of the canal. She kicks hard, swimming after it, then dives. The penny goes from copper to silvery blue as she chases it through the water. Bubbles tickle her lips. She's down ten feet when she catches up with the coin and grabs it.

She turns toward the sky and kicks. The cool air hits her face. She's panting hard, trying to catch her breath, when she remembers the noise she heard last night: a gritty scrape, like the sound the *Martina*'s hatch makes sliding open. A minute later an engine fired up. It sounded like the Captain's moped, but it couldn't have been. He quit sneaking out at night. It was part of his promise to pay more attention to her.

She opens her hand. The penny glints brightly on her palm. "Tell me the truth, oh magic penny. Heads he snuck out, tails he didn't." She tosses the coin, catches it, and slaps it against her arm.

Heads.

"How about two out of three?" She quickly tosses and catches the coin twice more. Heads…and…heads. "You lie!" she tells honest Abe. "I checked this morning. The moped was *exactly* where he parked it after work. What do you know anyway? You're just a dumb penny."

She holds her arm out over the water. "See ya, Abe." And she lets the penny go. She watches it drift through the layers of water—the silver, the green, the deep blue—until it disappears in the murky dark. "Put that with the others," she says softly.

As the daughter of a world-famous marine biologist, she knows that very little lives in the deepest part of the canal. Most living things need light. But she sometimes imagines another girl down there, stretching up a hand to catch the penny.

The water girl's pale hand is closing over the coin when Aunt Emma steps onto the back deck of the marina office in a stretchy pink sweat suit and sneakers. She's come out to do shrimp duty. "You still in the water?" she asks, reaching for the dip net.

"No." Mica lazily treads water.

"Too much sun is bad for your skin, you know." Aunt Emma stands by the tank, skimming off the dead shrimp that float at the top. When Mica does shrimp duty she rests her arms on the cool lip of the tank and studies the shrimp clustered by the bubbler. Aunt Emma pays no attention to live shrimp—just dead ones. What Mica and her father call "wildlife" Aunt Emma calls "bait."

It would be different if Anna were here. They would both lean on the edge of the tank and observe the shrimp. Mica would show Anna how to sneak a hand into the foam and how, with a single touch, you can make a shrimp jet across the tank. She'd tell her how these same pink shrimp ride the tide that runs through Snake Creek from ocean to bay and back again—at least until something eats them. Anna would be interested.

Aunt Emma dumps the dead shrimp over the railing. "There go the profits!" she jokes. Pelicans waiting in the water fight over them. Aunt Emma doesn't notice the pelicans any more than she does the shrimp. "Mica, honey, did you put on sunscreen?"

"Uh-huh." She would've said it stronger if it were true.

"When, last week? Better climb out and put some on," Aunt Emma calls as she goes back inside.

Mica dives, acting as if she hasn't heard, and swims underwater. With each stroke she feels her hair pulse back, then cloud around her as the water slows her down. As she propels herself toward the shallow water beside the dock she composes a letter in her head: *Dear Anna...Sorry it took me so long to write back...*

Anna's letter came a week ago. Since then Mica's written lots of answers—but only in her head. As she swims she looks up at the mirror surface of the water. Just ahead, something long and skinny pierces the water. It bobs as she swims toward it. Of course she knows what it is—she sees them all the time.

Not Anna though. Anna's probably never seen one, ever. Mica reaches up and grabs it. *Perfect*, she thinks, boosting herself up onto the deck.

"Paper!" she yells as she trots into the office. "I need paper!" She waits impatiently for Aunt Emma to dig through a musty drawer in the marina's file cabinet, a puddle forming under her bare feet. "Paper and a towel."

Mica dries off fast and sits on the towel. The ends of her hair drip on the paper. The spots on the page will dry before she sticks it in the envelope, leaving little salty rings.

Dear Anna,

Sorry it took me so long to write back—I wanted to send something extra-good.

Answers to questions first: I sleep in the V-berth at the bow. In case you don't know, the bow is the pointy front end of the boat. There's one bunk against each wall with a wedge-shaped space in between. Sleeping aboard is way different from sleeping in a house. The boat tugs at the ropes, the ropes creak, water slaps the hull. A boat feels alive.

Not to hurt your feelings, but a house just sits there sticking out of the ground. You can't take a trip in a house or catch fish from a house. You can't dive off a house (I climb the mast and jump from twenty feet up—ask Ben). And you definitely can't snorkel under a house. A three-foot barracuda I named Mr. Needles lives under the <u>Martina.</u> You should see his teeth! He only looks scary, though. He's a total wuss. He won't bother me unless I wear something shiny. To a barracuda any shiny flash is a minnow. And when a barracuda sees a minnow, it sees lunch. I always take my necklace off before I jump in the water.

I agree with you about animals. They <u>all</u> have emotions. I've observed it. And if you observe something repeatedly, science says it's true. The Captain just read what I wrote. He says to tell you that animal brains are too simple to generate emotions. But lots of stupid people have emotions. I've observed <u>that</u> plenty of times too. The Captain agrees about stupid people—but he still says I'm wrong about animals.

I'm in my room now. The Captain kept looking over my shoulder.

Do I feel lonely? I guess sometimes. But I make friends fast—like Ben and Cody. The three of us did everything together while they were here. We were like glue until they had to go home. At first I missed them. I'm over it now.

When no kids are around I hang out in the marina office and do my schoolwork. (The Captain checks it later.) Aunt Emma says she forgot all that stuff long ago. But she encourages me with chips and soda. In the middle of the day we watch soap operas on the TV behind the counter.

I'm in charge when she dozes off. I pump gas and run the register. When Uncle Bert yells for a cold soda I take it out to him (Uncle Bert is <u>always</u> under the awning on the side of the shop messing around with engines). When he yells, "Where's my third hand?" that means he needs me to hold a flashlight or hand him a tool. But most of the time I'm in the office with Aunt Emma.

You're probably wondering about the strange thing I sent you. Aunt Emma calls it a sea dagger. It's a seed from a red mangrove (<u>Rhizophora mangle</u>). There are three kinds of mangroves: red, black, and white. Reds grow right in the water on long, skinny roots. Ben and Cody thought they looked like spiders marching into the sea. The roots catch anything that floats by and turn it into land—red mangroves are island builders. Once they've made some safe solid land, the black mangroves move in. If the blacks do okay, then the wimpy white mangroves take root. By then the red mangroves are farther out in the water. Reds are the explorers.

Stick this seed in a glass of water. If it made the trip okay it should grow. Trying to build an island in a glass in Tallahassee, it will be the bravest red mangrove yet.

Is Ben Floyd cute? Pa-leeze. He's a total mess on the water. When he swims he just flops around. He thinks that diving means pulling up your knees and jumping. I worked on him as much as I could but he's a lost cause.

His brother Cody is sweet. But don't <u>ever</u> catch a fish in front of him! He'll make you throw it back. He doesn't understand about the food chain. We're at the top. Fish are near the bottom. If a person catches a fish they're <u>supposed</u> to eat it—as long as it's not rare or anything. Ben and Cody's family eats fish but not meat. Instead of meat their mom cooks this fake rubbery stuff called tofu—Cody calls it toad food but a toad wouldn't like it either.

Do you eat fish or are you a cow person? The Captain and I are omnivores—we eat anything as long as it comes in a can. But between fish and cow, I think it's better to eat fish. A fish lives free until someone catches it. Where do cows live free?

Your Sorta Sister,
Mica

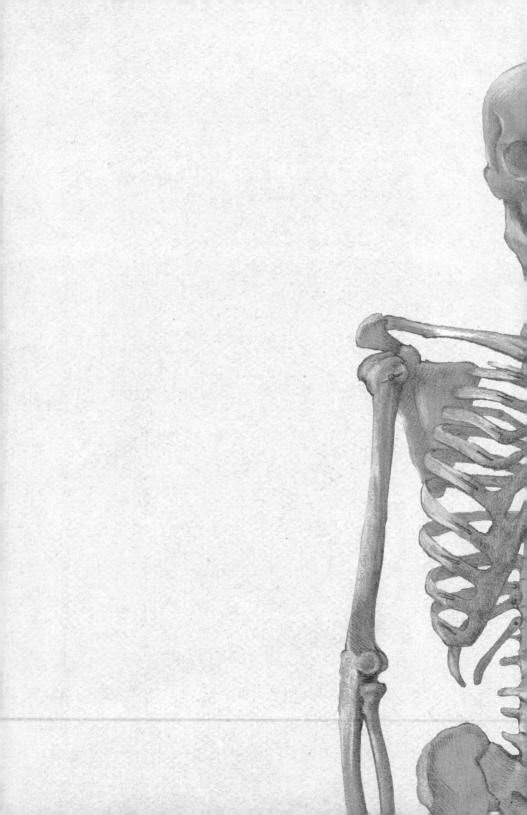

chapter 4

"INDIA!" MISS J SAYS, THUMPING the latest letter posted on the refrigerator with her knuckle.

Anna glances up from the blank paper on the table in front of her. "India?"

"Mica asked where cows live free. Well, that's the place. It's a crime to kill a cow in India. They're sacred."

"You mean like, 'Holy cow'?"

Miss J laughs her usual big laugh, then points at the paper in front of Anna. "What're you writing?"

"So far, nothing." Anna slumps over the empty page. "I have to figure out what to do for my English assignment."

"Oh, right. Homework." The chair opposite Anna's complains as Miss J falls into it. That reminds Anna of Aunt Betsy's "sitting lessons." When *ladies* sit they lower themselves—with dignity—then cross their ankles. Even though she practiced, Anna never did it right. Maybe her unladylikeness was what made Aunt Betsy give her away. Luckily with Miss J she's home free. When it comes to sitting, Miss J just drops.

Miss J slings a leg up. The heel of her old army boot rests on the table edge. "Guess I should get to work too." She picks some seeds off her purple sock. "I'm procrastinating again, aren't I? Setting a bad example. Don't tell Mrs. Riley!"

Anna would never tell the social worker anything to mess up her placement—but Miss J *does* tend to procrastinate. "What's *your* homework?" Anna offers her a pencil.

Miss J takes it—and tosses it up in the air. "I have to lesson-plan a unit on locomotion in single-cell animals," she says, catching the pencil just before it hits the table. "Yours?"

"A two-page essay titled 'My Favorite Place.'"

Miss J tosses the pencil again, then lunges over the table, almost punching Anna in her hurry to catch it. "Close one! Sorry! What place did you choose?"

Anna points to the blank page.

"Must be hard, you've lived so many places."

Anna pulls her feet up onto the chair and hugs her knees. "Sometimes I imagine there's a me in each of those places, still living all those different lives."

"Interesting." Miss J props her elbows and the table creaks. "A dozen Annas."

Anna grins. "Scary, isn't it?"

"Heck no! More Annas to go around! What's the first place you remember?"

Anna wishes she remembered the house she lived in with her parents, but she was too little. She remembers the second house, though. "My grandmother's…" She closes her eyes to see it better. "There was a rocking chair we used to sit in together." Anna opens her eyes again. "But a rocking chair isn't a place, is it?"

"Sure it is. Growing up, *my* favorite place was under the porch steps. Except for me and the dog, no one even noticed it. If a shady spot under the steps is a place, why not a chair?"

Anna shrugged.

"So tell me about this chair." Miss J crosses her arms behind her head and leans back.

But all Anna can recall is the soothing motion of the rocker and being in her grandmother's lap. Even Grandma's face is hard to picture. The silvery-thin memory scares her. Shouldn't she remember her own grandmother perfectly and forever? She looks up at Miss J and wonders how quickly she would forget Miss J's face if she had to leave. Never, she decides, but she's not sure. Memory is not the safest place to keep the people you love.

"Maybe I could write about the stream behind Uncle Charles's house," Anna says, choosing the first place that comes into her head. "Me and my cousins used to wade in it all the time. We'd pick up stones and spook crayfish."

Her aunt and uncle's was the last place she lived before she got dumped into foster care. She was sure that she'd stay with them forever, but then they got divorced. She still misses Uncle Charles and her cousins, even Aunt Eva, who yelled in Spanish when she got mad—and you didn't have to understand Spanish to know what she was saying.

It makes her sad to think about them, so Anna concentrates on the stream. "The water was icy cold."

"Bet it was spring fed. A stream's a good favorite place."

"Wait!" Why didn't she think of it before? "My real, real favorite is this house."

Miss J looks up, surprised. "Our house?"

As a smile breaks on her foster mom's face, Anna mentally adds the word "our" to her secret proof list. The telescope is already on the list. So is the dog Miss J let her pick out at the pound.

"I don't know…" Miss J swivels around in her chair. "Things are kind of mix and match." No two pieces of china on the shelf over the sink are the same pattern. "And the dogs have worn out the linoleum over there by the stove. Funny that Beauty picked the same spot where Gregor used to like to lie down."

"It's not worn out, exactly. More like loved."

"They've loved the pattern right off it! I'm just saying, our house isn't very fancy."

"*Our* house is the most interesting house in the world."

"Some folks would call it an unholy mess."

"It's not a mess, it's a museum!"

"A messy museum." Miss J flips the pencil so high the point makes a dot on the ceiling. "Oops! You think I should get up on a chair and erase that?"

Anna's not sure the creaky chair could take Miss J climbing up on it. "Leave it. It looks like a tiny black star."

Miss J closes one eye and gazes at the ceiling. "I guess what you see depends on how you look at it."

"True."

Looking around the kitchen, Anna chooses to see the four jars of feathers on the back of the stove (some iridescent), and the carton of rare (possibly valuable) fossils shoved up against the wall, and the half dozen nests on top of the refrigerator (one no bigger than a tablespoon and held together with spiderweb).

Anna rests a hand on the rock that sits in the middle of the table. This chunk of karst, a piece of the limestone bedrock that underlies most of the area, is at the very top of her proof list. She and Miss J collected it when they were waiting to hear if Social Services would let her live with Miss J. When the answer came back "yes," they put the rock in the middle of the table and vowed to keep it there forever.

They call it the "Staying Rock."

Anna picks up her own pencil and writes: In my house (my favorite place) I have a big, very special rock on my kitchen table.

But a big rock—even a special one—isn't what you'd find on a normal kitchen table.

She watches Miss J, who is *finally* doing her homework. One hand writes, the other tugs at the sandy blond ponytail that's held back with a twist tie. Miss J doesn't spend money on frivolous things like hair clips. Why bother when the twist tie works just as well?

Miss J and this house go together. *Miss J, this house, and me,* Anna thinks. At least most of the time. There's no string of Annas living in all the places from her past, but there *are* two Annas: home-Anna and school-Anna. Home-Anna (her real self) doesn't like school-Anna much, but why get school-Anna in trouble by writing something that her classmates will think is weird? They think she's weird enough already. "Erasing!" she announces.

Like the chairs, the table wobbles. If Anna or Miss J writes while the other erases, the words turn to wild scribbles, so even though she's in the middle of a word, Miss J lifts her pencil point.

As Anna erases, the Staying Rock clicks against the table. She erases until the paper gets furry, then turns her pencil back over—and can't think of a thing to write.

Miss J stretches and yawns a big yawn. "It's happy hour at Goodwill. Anything on a hanger is two-for-one. Want to go look?"

"Sure." Anna drops her pencil. Before getting up she leans across the table and points at the half-word on Miss J's paper. "What's a "flage"?"

Miss J picks up her pencil just long enough to write "lla," then shoves the pencil through the top of her ponytail for safe-keeping. "Not 'flage.' Flagella."

"What's a flagella?"

"It's more than one flagellum. Tell you about it on the way. Now, where did I stick my danged wallet?"

As they back out of the driveway, Miss J steers her Volkswagen Bug one-handed while demonstrating the motion of flagella with the other. "A flagellum is the whiplike part on some protozoans—you know, those little single-cell guys. It moves them around. I'll show you in the microscope when we get home."

"Great!" Anna wonders if any other girl in her class would be excited about seeing flagella. "Do you think Mica knows about flagella?"

"Bet she does. After all, she lives with Dr. Robin Michael Delano."

"The World-famous Marine Biologist!" they chant together.

They say that every time one of them mentions Mica's dad—and then they laugh. Miss Johnette calls people who think a lot of themselves "puffy." It might not be fair; they don't even know him. But after reading Mica's letter they agree: Dr. Robin Michael Delano—the World-famous Marine Biologist—is puffy.

Anna feels sort of bad for laughing at him. But he'll never know, and it's something she and her foster mom can laugh about that no one else understands.

Anna's lived in enough places to know that sharing a secret joke is one of the ways you can tell who's part of a family. Anyone who doesn't know the joke is just visiting.

Johnette watches Anna's eyes more closely than the passing parade of sweatshirts. "How about this one?" she asks, pushing another hanger along the rack. "Orange is a great color."

Anna picks up a strand of her own hair and wraps it around a finger, something Johnette's noticed she does when she's uncertain. "It's…okay."

"Right. I forget you're not an orange person." She grabs the hanger and slides it along the rod, fast. *There's got to be something here that Anna likes,* Johnette thinks. *We just have to replace Janice Casey's sorry old sweater.* "It's hard to believe people give away all this great stuff, isn't it?"

"Except this one." Anna stops the parade to point out a sweatshirt with rubber cherries glued to it. "This one deserved to be given away."

"Or burned." Johnette is quick to push the hanger aside. "Hey!" she whoops as the next sweatshirt comes into view. "Look at this one!" She jerks it off the hanger and holds it up to Anna's narrow shoulders. "Check out the wolves! And look what it says: 'Support the Wilderness Society.' This is *so* great. You stay warm and at the same time you're a walking billboard for conservation."

"Miss Ja–ay!"

"Wow! You used that whiny voice kids use when they can't believe what their crazy mothers are doing."

Anna falters. "I didn't mean to sound whiny."

"No, no. Whiny is good. Next time roll your eyes."

Anna tries an eye roll.

"Perfect!" Johnette gives Anna a one-armed hug. "Now tell me, what's wrong with the sweatshirt?"

Anna grabs the sides and wraps them around herself.

"I get it. Too big. The wolf pack meets itself in the back."

"But look." Anna turns it around. "It's perfect for you." She holds the wolf pack up to her foster mom's chest. "No wrapping, see? The whole pack shows."

"I already have a sweatshirt."

"I know. The one with prairie dogs. But this one's only three dollars."

"Even that's too much for something I don't need."

"Two sweatshirts aren't so many. Most people have lots and lots. Let's say we're camping and your prairie dogs get wet."

Johnette decides to play along. "And let's say we were hiking in Alaska so we can't go home."

"And let's say it's cold," Anna adds. "Frigid."

"Glacial." Johnette wraps both arms around the shirt. "Don't even *try* to talk me out of this shirt. I *have* to buy it. My life depends on it." She drapes the shirt over her shoulder. "But you'll be on that trip too, and you don't even have one warm sweatshirt."

"True." Anna begins leafing through the rack herself. "No...no...*really* no. This one looks like it's covered with cottage cheese."

"Or baby puke," adds Johnette. "And a big no on that one," she says, nixing the next sweatshirt in line. "There are some ugly specimens here today, aren't there?" Johnette wonders if, for once, she should break her "reuse everything" rule and take Anna to the mall.

She's about to suggest it when Anna gasps and grabs the sleeve of a fleecy blue sweatshirt. "Look!"

"'Girls Just Wanna Have Fun'?" Johnette says, reading the front. "Wouldn't you rather have one with a good old mammal on it?" Then, seeing Anna hugging the shirt as if it were a favorite blanket, she wants to shoot herself. "But that one would be good and warm—and hey, why shouldn't girls have fun?"

Anna strokes the soft fabric with her fingertips. "It looks like the shirts the girls in my class wear."

"Plus it seems brand-new."

Miss J whips it off the hanger and holds it up to Anna's shoulders. But Anna picks up a sleeve. "Too bad there's a stain on the elbow."

"Imagine giving away a brand-new sweatshirt because of one little stain."

Anna takes a long hard look at it. "I bet it's too small to notice. Smaller than a ladybug." She grins at Johnette, showing her chipped front tooth—*something else we'd better fix,* thinks Johnette. "It's smaller than a flagellum."

"Speaking of which…" Johnette slings an arm around Anna's neck. "Let's go home and look at some. With your sweatshirt and mine we have our two-for-one." She blows her breath out hard. "I absolutely hate to shop."

"Me too. Definitely."

"In fact, I would rather stand in a fire-ant mound."

She can tell Anna wants to agree but wants to be truthful. "Shopping's not *that* bad. It's at least ten percent better than standing in a fire-ant mound."

By the next afternoon Anna wishes she'd never seen the blue sweatshirt. In fact, if she could, she would take her whole day at school, crush it into a ball, and throw it in the garbage.

But sometimes the best way to forget is to tell someone. She's putting everything in a letter to Mica—all the gory details. Behind her on the roof she hears Miss Johnette's whistling and the scratch of the broom across the shingles, but she's absorbed in the letter.

The whistling and sweeping stop. "Shouldn't you get back from that edge a little?" Miss J calls.

"I'm fine." Anna sits with her legs hanging over, her school notebook open in her lap.

"Of course you are." Miss J goes back to sweeping. "You take after me when it comes to heights. Do you think being a mom is making me worry about things that aren't problems?"

"Uh-huh."

"Hey." The broom stops in midsweep. "You're wearing your cousin's sweater again. What happened to 'Girls Just Wanna Have Fun'?"

Anna keeps her head down. "Took it off when I got home from school."

"Get any compliments, like, 'Cool sweatshirt'?"

Anna wraps a strand of hair around her finger. "They noticed."

"They noticed?" Miss J rests the broom against her shoulder and puts her knuckles on her hips. "Good noticed or bad noticed?"

"Ashlee said she used to have one just like it." Anna leans back on her arms and feels the sun on her face. "It's nice up here on the roof."

"Amen to that!" Miss J pushes a pile of leaves off the roof. Anna watches them whirl to the ground. Miss J peers over her shoulder. "You doing homework?"

"No." Anna slides her arm over the page. "Writing to Mica."

"If you want something to send her, I have the perfect thing." Miss J steps sideways up the roof. "Why don't you send her this?" She reaches down and grabs something. "Bet she's never seen anything like it. We'll need a sturdy box to pack it in."

"And instructions on how to bring it back to life."

Dear Mica,

Last night I was supposed to write about "my favorite place" for English class (two pages). I wanted to write about the house we live in. It's like a museum. (Miss J has been collecting stuff all her life.) The oldest specimens are insects she collected when she was a kid. She netted them, then put them in killing jars with nail polish remover. I bet they were beautiful, but carpet beetles got in the boxes and ruined them. After that she decided that you don't need to kill things to collect them.

She's found plenty of bugs since then (and I found some), but we only collect them if they're dead already. Most of the animal bones and skulls used to be roadkill. We keep dermestid beetles to clean them. Sometimes we find the bones in the woods, clean and dry and already picked over by vultures and insects. We gather arrowheads and fossils along riverbeds. A life-size human skeleton named Edgar hangs in our closet. He's only a plastic reproduction, but the bones make a great rattling sound when you open the door. I could have written a hundred pages about our house, but it seemed safer to write about the mall. I hope Miss J never reads what I wrote. She calls malls "black holes."

Warning! The crunchy curled-up stuff on the branch I sent only looks dead. It's a bunch of resurrection ferns. Drying up is the trick they do to survive when there isn't enough rain. Miss J said the ferns only grow on live oaks and you don't have them down there.

It seems like all oaks should be called "live," but Miss J says the live oak got its name because it keeps its leaves all winter—then drops and replaces them in a hurry. They're not falling yet, but we're getting ready for them. That's why I'm writing you from the roof. Miss J and I are sweeping the old leaves off. It's her turn with the broom.

I can see why you like your boat, but I like our house. The roof is one of the good things about it. Miss J and I bring blankets up here some nights. We lie on our backs and watch meteors and satellites through the branches of a huge live oak we call the Old Senator. The dead branch with the fern on it was lying on the roof when we got up here. The O.S. will never miss it. Three people with their arms stretched can barely touch fingers around its trunk. Big trees are another good thing about living on land. Specifically, climbing big trees.

If I homeschooled I'd study in the tree. Trees are good company. Better than some people. In my tree-school there would be no Ashlee Burns. Why not, you ask? Here is just one reason: Today Ashlee asked where I got my new sweatshirt. I said Goodwill. She showed everyone a stain on the elbow that proved it used to be hers. Then her friend Madison said, "You shop at Goodwill?" (Miss J and I shop there all the time. If you reuse things instead of throwing them away, you help the environment.) Ashlee said she wouldn't go to school in somebody else's nasty stained-up sweatshirt if it saved the whole universe.

When they get to high school they'll have Miss J for biology. Hopefully she'll convince them to reuse things and conserve. But until then they think I'm wearing someone else's garbage.

Your SS, Anna

p.s. To bring the fern back to life just add water.

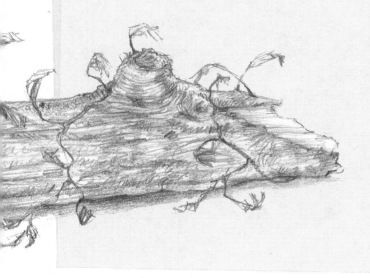

chapter 5

"DONE." MICA DROPS HER PENCIL on the page of geometry problems.

"Goodness! A whole day's worth of schoolwork done in two hours and…" Aunt Emma looks over her shoulder and checks the clock "…fourteen minutes."

"Yes!" Mica thrusts her arms over her head. "A new personal best! The old record was two hours and seventeen, remember?"

"I'll take your word for it." Aunt Emma tucks the last page into Mica's schoolwork folder. Although Aunt Emma can never help with her assignments, Mica appreciates the way she keeps them from getting lost or snack-stained or doodled on. Aunt Emma slides the folder into the "Invoices" drawer of the old metal file cabinet. "You're free for the rest of the day, so what do you want to do next?"

Mica blinks as she realizes there's nothing she wants to do next. She can't swim. During the night the weather snapped cold. She fished from the *Martina*'s deck just after the sun came up, so she doesn't feel like fishing. They never turn the TV on until it's time for their soaps, and reading is too much like school. She took her Zodiac, the small inflated boat the Captain gave her for her ninth birthday, out yesterday. And that's all she can think of.

She lowers her head until her cheek rests on the glass countertop. She's concentrating on the chill of the smooth surface when Aunt Emma suggests a bag of chips. "To celebrate your personal best."

Mica just shakes her head, swiping the glass with her cheek. Suddenly she's tired of everything. Even chips.

"What's wrong, honey?"

"Nothing. I'm just bored."

Aunt Emma strokes her hair. "If only you were in school," she says softly, then gives Mica's shoulder a brisk pat. "I know! A nice game of gin rummy might cheer you up."

But Mica doesn't lift her head. They've played gin rummy almost every day since Ben and Cody left. The pennies they bet flow back and forth between her jar and Aunt Emma's like the tide. They never get spent. The only time one disappears is when Mica lets it drift to the bottom of the canal and into the open hand of the girl she almost believes is waiting there.

"You don't want chips. You don't want to play rummy." She hears Aunt Emma's fingertips tap the glass. "Shall I see if Uncle Bert has any little jobs for you?"

But Mica has decided that she'll never lift her head again, at least not until someone gives her a good reason—one that's way better than holding a flashlight for Uncle Bert.

Behind her there's a scuffling noise as someone hurries into the office.

"Captain Delano! What a surprise." Mica can hear the relief in Aunt Emma's voice—she'd probably figured out that Mica planned to rest her head on the sales counter forever. "Aren't you supposed to be at Fun Camp?"

"My next group won't be there for forty minutes," he says quickly. "I have news!"

Mica jolts up from the counter and turns toward him. "What news?"

There's a spot of pink on each of his cheeks and his chest is heaving. He must have jumped off the bike and run as fast as his bad leg allowed. But now that he's here, Mica can tell the Captain is enjoying the suspense. The pith helmet he holds by its brim turns around and around in his hands.

"Tell!" she commands.

His eyes sparkle. "You sure you wouldn't like to guess?" The hat stops spinning and he grins at her. "All right. Time's up." Still, he waits a little longer, as if the words are building up behind his smile. "It seems that one of my grants has come through."

"Yes!" Mica jumps off her stool and plows into her father, rocking him with the force of her hug.

He pats her on the back. "No need to get carried away."

"Yes there is!" She bursts out of the awkward hug and does a cartwheel between the shelves of motor oil. She lands on her feet, breathing hard. "You can quit Biology Fun Camp and go back to your real work! Which grant, sea grass or bivalves?"

"Sea grass. The one I applied for with Dr. Winn—he pulled a few strings and got it."

Mica doesn't like Dr. Winn. He's old, and he thinks she's a nuisance, not a scientist-in-training. He has hair in his nose. But if he pulled strings for her father, she'll give him a second chance.

"We'll be working out of his lab in Marathon."

"Hooray! We have a lab again!" Doing science on the picnic table is not very dignified for a world-famous marine biologist and his scientist-in-training assistant. "It's a year-long grant, right?"

"With possible extensions."

She spins toward the counter. "That means we can stay! A year at least—longer with extensions!" She makes a run at Aunt Emma, who opens her arms.

"What wonderful news!" Aunt Emma folds her arms around Mica. "Of course you'll stay right here. I couldn't part with my girl!"

"You're sure you don't mind?" her father asks. "Mica must be inconvenient sometimes." His excitement seems to be evaporating. He sounds like his usual self.

"Look at us!" Mica says. "We're hugging here! She likes me!" Mica gazes at Aunt Emma. "You like me, right?"

Aunt Emma smooths Mica's bangs off her forehead. "Of course I do, honey." But the Captain acts as if the hug display is happening on some other planet.

When a horn sounds down at the dock Mica says, "I'll get it!" and dashes out the door to pump gas for whoever just pulled up. She'll show her father how much in the way she is.

A skiff idles at the gas dock. Wiley Millman's at the wheel. His dog, Jethro, occupies the stern seat. As Mica trots through the blue exhaust of the idling engine, the dog bounds to the dock and plants his paws on her chest. "Not now, boy. I have a job to do." After a quick pat she pushes him away. "Gas, Mr. Millman?"

"Nope. Today I need shrimp." Mr. Millman swings his bait bucket over to her. "Give me a couple dozen big boys—and get in the back, Jethro!"

She pads up the wooden steps. She's reaching for the dip net that hangs on a nail above the tank when she hears Aunt Emma's voice. "This is the perfect opportunity to send her to school, Dr. Delano."

Mica forgets the net in her hand.

"*Public* school?" The Captain is using his you-must-be-kidding voice. "You want me to enroll her in *public* school? She's so far ahead. What could they possibly teach her?"

"School isn't just about learning. It's social too. It's about making friends," Aunt Emma insists. "It's about doing things girls her age are supposed to do."

"Such as?"

"How should I know? I'm an old lady. I love her to death, but she needs friends her own age."

"May I point out that it's the middle of February? The school year is more than half over."

Wiley yells up from the gas dock, "Those shrimp givin' ya trouble? They fightin' back?"

Mica scrapes the net along the side of the tank fast, dislodging shrimp. She lifts the dripping net out of the water, pushes the spring-loaded door of the bait bucket back, and dumps the shrimp. She fills the net a couple more times, giving him two dozen, more or less.

The bait bucket sloshes as she jogs it over to the gas dock. "That'll be four fifty."

He passes her a five.

"Be right back with your change, Mr. Millman."

"Keep it," he says with a wink. "We wanna get out there sometime today, don't we, Jethro?" He tips his ball cap to her, then nudges the throttle forward and leaves her standing in a blue fog.

As she breathes in the smell of unburned gasoline—a smell she sort of likes—she thinks about sneaking back up and listening in on the school conversation. Instead she studies the frayed cuffs on the oversized sweatshirt she's wearing. No point in even thinking about school. She hasn't been in regular school since first grade. Why would the Captain let her go now?

She flops down on the dock between the *Martina* and Aunt Emma and Uncle Bert's houseboat. Legs dangling, she rests one foot on the gray rubber gunwale of her Zodiac, which is tethered off the stern of the sailboat. With a kick—*poing*—she sends it swinging out across the water. It stops with a lurch when it reaches the end of its rope. While she waits for the wind to push it back, she compares the two bigger boats.

Restless at the dock, their sailboat bobs in the slight breeze. The *Martina* is a migratory bird that lights for a moment and then moves on. It's named after her mother. Mica feels for the heaviest thing on the chain around her neck—her mother's wedding ring. It rests cold in her hand. She gives the Zodiac another sharp kick—*poing*—then turns toward Aunt Emma and Uncle Bert's houseboat.

The Love Boat sits perfectly still. The Captain calls houseboats "floating trailers." But with its lace curtains, front porch, and hanging flower baskets, it reminds Mica of a real house. She lived in one the last time she went to school.

The Zodiac swings in again. She presses her arches against its warm rubber and tries to remember school.

What she remembers is Danielle Paterno.

They used to play together at recess, share things out of their lunch boxes. Danielle wore long black braids and a blue sweater with kittens on the front.

Mica leans back on her arms. It's not that she doesn't have friends now—she has plenty. Their pictures are all over the walls of her V-berth. The second she sees a boat docking with a kid or two on board she introduces herself.

But how often has she jumped out of her berth and run to the slip where friends were docked just the night before, only to find empty water? She's learned to snap their pictures right away.

After a while, though, the photos become the memory. Even Ben and Cody, who were just here, are beginning to look only like their pictures. She can't see them doing anything but making the same stupid faces she saw through the viewfinder when she photographed them.

She feels inside the deep pouch in the front of Uncle Bert's sweatshirt (borrowed off a hook in the store). Her fingers close around the special leaf she intends to send Anna. Anna could be a friend for a long, long time. But it's hard to have a best friend whose voice you've never heard, whose face you've never seen. Mica doesn't even have a picture of her.

Even though it was way back in first grade, she remembers Danielle Paterno perfectly. She'd like to have a friend like that again.

But by now the Captain and Aunt Emma are probably talking about the weather. Blah, blah, blah. Even though they can't do a thing about it, adults talk about weather all the time, especially the Captain.

She gives the Zodiac another kick. This time, just as she looks up, her father lurches down the office steps. She watches him approach out of the tops of her eyes. He pauses to check out the fern Anna sent. It sits on the railing, dried up again and completely dead-looking.

He limps down the steps and along the dock. The Captain swims better than anyone, but out of water he jerks around like a fish flopping in the bottom of a boat. When he finally gets to where she's sitting, he doesn't say a thing. He wraps an arm around a piling and lowers himself to the dock, drawing a sharp breath through his teeth. Sitting down is hard since his bad knee won't bend. Her heart *ga-thunk*s. Sitting means they're going to have a "meeting of the board."

But when he's finally seated, one leg sticking out stiff over the water, he still doesn't say anything.

She can't stand the silence. "Meeting of the board?" she asks.

"Yes. Called to order. Aunt Emma thinks you should go to public school."

She watches him warily through her thicket of bangs.

"Would you like to?" He keeps his eyes on the flag over the Coast Guard station.

She would. She definitely would. But she's sure he wants her to say no. That's why he's not looking at her. "What do *you* think?" she asks.

"You know the rules." He crosses his arms. "Since this primarily affects you, you have the deciding vote." At the most important times he's no help at all—but that doesn't mean he won't find a way to make a comment. Now he points out a clump of sponges on one of the houseboat's mooring ropes. "There's a clear sign a boat's been in one place for too long."

He's reminding her that staying put might be good enough for other people, but not for them. Mica glances up from the sponge-covered ropes and stares longingly at Aunt Emma's lace curtains. "We'll be here for a year anyway."

"So," he says, suddenly brisk. "You want to go to school."

"I think I do…"

"You *think* you do?"

She squares her shoulders. "I mean, yes sir. I do."

"Hanging around with your old dad isn't very exciting, is it?" he says softly.

"That's not it. It's just that you're hardly ever here."

"You could have come with me to Fun Camp."

She picks a splinter of wood off the dock. "I went last year. It was boring. I know all that stuff already."

"All right. It's probably for the best. I'll be busy at the lab anyway."

Suddenly it's like she's a junk fish he's caught, a grunt or a saltwater cat—something not good enough to keep so he's throwing her back. "I don't *have* to go to school," she says quickly. "I won't if you want me to help with the grant. I could go with you like we did with the last sea grass study, remember?"

"I don't think Dr. Winn would approve."

"But it's your grant!"

"His and mine. And it's his lab." The corners of his eyes crinkle. "And maybe Aunt Emma's right. You need some friends your own age. You're like the fern that girl in Tallahassee sent. All shriveled up and waiting for rain."

Mica pushes the side of the Zodiac down with one foot until a little cool water slides over her bare toes and into the boat. "Okay. But it's only 'til we leave here—"

"All settled then." He slaps his thighs. "Meeting adjourned."

"Hey, guess what!" she says as he struggles to his feet. She grasps the leg of his khaki pants and hangs on. "I'm cooking your favorite supper. Ravioli!"

He looks down at her. "Guess I'd better enjoy your cooking while I can."

She wraps both arms around his legs. "Nothing's going to change because of school. I'm *still* the family cook."

"Saying you cook may be an exaggeration."

She rests her chin on his knees and looks up at him. "I cook better than you!"

"True. You're the world's best can-opener chef."

She lets go of his legs and kneels. "I know! To celebrate we'll eat ravioli and then we'll work on the puzzle."

"To tell you the truth, I'm a little tired of that puzzle. It's silly, don't you think? Someone cuts up a picture and we have to put it back together."

She jumps to her feet. "We *have* to finish it." The two-thousand-piece puzzle is spread all over the table in the galley (their only table). She's a little tired of it too, but can't admit it. It's their father-daughter project. So far they've done the border and one mountain. Last night she found a piece in the sink stuck to the bottom of a pan.

"Go inside and relax for a few minutes." She walks backward. "I have to give Aunt Emma the money for Mr. Millman's shrimp. Then we'll eat and we'll puzzle."

He pulls himself up onto the deck of the *Martina,* then turns toward her. "Suggestion: Why don't we toss the darned thing overboard and let the fish put it together?"

She points a finger at him. "Don't you *dare* dump that puzzle." And she runs down the dock toward the office. Aunt Emma is standing in the door, beaming.

Just in case the Captain's watching, they retreat to the office before they high-five. Aunt Emma is ecstatic. "You're going to school!"

Mica hugs herself. "I know!"

"Of course the Captain will have to get your records from the correspondence school. And your shots will have to be up to date."

"Shots?"

"And you'll need some new clothes, and I'll call my hairdresser, Angie, and make you an emergency hair appointment." Mica has never really liked Aunt Emma's hair. It's frizzy and a hard-to-believe orangey brown.

"I bet they'll like me as is." Then she remembers Anna's letter and looks down at her as-is sweatshirt. "New clothes would be okay, I guess." She's about to say that her hair is just fine when she hears the sound of the moped starting. Where's he going? She reaches the door in time to see her father cut across the parking lot as fast as a bottle rocket and jet onto US 1.

Her fingernails bite into her palms. He couldn't be... Two

weeks ago he promised her he wouldn't go there again. A promise doesn't expire in two weeks. The moped buzzes across Snake Creek Bridge. Maybe he's going to the Townsite Shopper to buy a cake or something. It's a big day for both of them.

"Cake," she whispers. "Get cake." But he takes a hard right into the parking lot of the bar on the other side of the bridge.

Aunt Emma joins her in the doorway. "I thought he quit all that." As the moped wobbles into a parking space, the Captain waves to someone at the outdoor bar.

"I…" Mica gulps. "I gotta go." Before her father walks down the dock to the waterside bar, before he orders his first drink, Mica twists away from the hand on her shoulder. Eyes burning, she runs down the dock.

She shoves the *Martina*'s hatch and falls into the cabin. His note sits inside the hollow square of the unfinished puzzle.

> Gone across the creek. Had to celebrate the good news about the grant with Dr. Winn. Don't worry. Will drink ginger ale only. Work your can-opener magic. Be back in half an hour.

"You could have celebrated with me!" She picks up a puzzle piece and tries to figure out where it goes, but it doesn't go anywhere—she can't even force it. "Stupid puzzle!" She sweeps all the pieces into the box lid and carries them up to the deck. When she spins, two thousand pieces scatter into the wind. A couple are caught by gulls before they can hit the water. The rest are still floating when she jumps back down into the cabin and rips a sheet of paper out of the sacred notebook the Captain calls his weather log.

Mica
was
here!

Dear Anna,

I don't want to celebrate alone (the Captain is out
somewhere) so I'm pretending you're here. We're in my cabin
sitting on the bunks. (Ignore the dirty laundry.)

Do you want to know why we're celebrating? The Captain
got a grant! (Cheers! Excitement!) Now he can quit teaching
kids who don't even like biology and go back to doing his
research. Usually I work with him but (GOOD NEWS!) Aunt
Emma wants me to go to public school. I'm going to try it.
(More cheers! More excitement!) Gulp... WISH ME LUCK!

It will take a few days to set things up. We have to get
paperwork from my correspondence school. I need shots
(ouch). And Aunt Emma thinks I need a haircut (double ouch).

The package you sent wouldn't fit in the post office box, so
we had to go to the window to pick it up. Aunt Emma got
all excited and made me open it right away. When she saw

the live oak branch with the ferns on it she wanted me to dump the whole thing in the trash. I read her your note but she didn't believe the resurrection part. She said it might have only been half-dead when you stuck it in the box, but the U.S. Postal Service killed it the rest of the way.
We hung it in the community shower while I washed my hair. By the time I had the shampoo rinsed out, the fern had resurrected! Aunt Emma called it a miracle. I told her it was just biology. She said that was too much to think about. She put the fern on the back deck in the sun. When it dried she resurrected it all over again for Uncle Bert. He thought it was a miracle too.

Are you wondering why I sent a leaf with my name on it? It's not just any old leaf. It's a leaf from an autograph tree (<u>Clusia rosea</u>).

Autograph trees hold their leaves even longer than live oaks. Conchs (what they call old time Keys people) used to scratch their names on autograph tree leaves at their friends' houses so they would remember them forever. I scratched mine into this leaf on our last stay at the marina. (I was only ten then. I don't dot my I's with hearts anymore.) My name was still there when we came back a year later.

When I picked the leaf for you, I signed another one right away in case I have to leave. That way Aunt Emma or anybody who walks by the tree will think of me. But maybe I won't have to leave. The Captain's grant is for a year at least. And sometimes grants get extended.

I'll try school, but if I don't like it and if Ashlee keeps bugging you, here is PLAN B: You come down here and homeschool with me. When we're done studying we can swim, snorkel, dive, watch the soaps. Miss J might let you come and stay until the end of the semester. Tell her the Sorta Sisters club is calling a meeting.

Gotta go. I hear the Captain's moped. Gotta cook supper presto.

Mica

chapter 6

WALKING HOME FROM SCHOOL, Anna shadows the usual kids from her neighborhood. Ben and Cass, Justin, Jemmie, and Leroy form a tight group a few paces ahead of her.

Leroy gives Justin a wedgie. "Man!" Justin shouts. "You are so dead!" He slaps Leroy on the back of the head. Jemmie tells them they're both immature. Ben and Cass swing their joined hands as they walk.

Anna imagines holding hands with someone, then catches herself swinging her own arm. How dumb did that look? Step by step she falls farther behind. No one notices.

Leroy rears his bike up on the back tire to impress Jemmie, but his bike is too small. If he sat on the seat his knees would hit the handlebars, so he stands and pedals in short, choppy strokes, circling the others. Justin says something about Leroy's clown bike. Leroy hops off and walks it. A handle grip with a plastic streamer rests against his hip. It's got to be his little brother's bike.

Anytime Leroy gets close to Jemmie, Justin steps closer to her too. Anna feels sorry for Justin. He's not tall like Leroy—the tiny bike would fit him fine. Plus he's heavy and his skin is pretty bad. But at least he's part of the group; at least he exists.

Last summer, when she first came to the neighborhood, she was part of the group too, but school puts a label on everyone. They're eighth graders, she's seventh. She's not in any of their classes. They don't mean to leave her out, but what do they have to talk about with her?

Anna puts her hands in her pockets so they don't look so useless and empty, and her fingers close over the leaf Mica sent in her last letter. It's thick and stiff like leather. She pulls it out and then takes a few quick steps to catch up. "Hey, Ben, I got another letter from your friend Mica."

Ben turns, swinging Cass around. Cass giggles, then pulls Ben up short, grabbing his hand in both of hers. "Is that the girl from the Keys?" She looks up into his eyes, even though she has to bend her knees to do it. "The one who *likes* you?"

"But I don't like her!" Ben protests.

"She doesn't like you either," Anna blurts out. "She says you can't swim or dive."

Ben turns red. "I swim fine. It's just that she's a fish. She has gills and everything."

"No she doesn't!" Anna's heart races—now she wishes she'd never mentioned the letter from Mica. She should quit talking but she opens her mouth and makes matters worse. "She doesn't even think you're cute."

"Who does?" Justin throws up both hands. "Poor Ben, nobody thinks he's cute."

"I do!" says Cass.

"Because you're blinded by *luv*," Leroy moans. Cass chases him.

Like leaves caught in a whirlwind, all the others follow. Anna watches them flurry away. Following slowly, she walks home alone.

As soon as she steps through the opening in the low stone wall that surrounds Miss J's house she feels better. Last summer the path to the door was crowded by flowers and the air was fuzzy with the hum of bees. Now that it's winter there are only a few snapdragons and pansies, some stiff milkweeds, and lots of plants so discouraged by the cold they've fallen over and turned brown. But Anna knows they'll come back; everything grows for Miss J.

She hooks the string around her neck with her pinkie and slides the key out of the neck of her T-shirt. At school she kept imagining she was far away from Tallahassee, in the marina office with Mica. But she couldn't really leave here. She'd miss all of this too much.

Claws scrabble on the inside of the door. "I'm coming, Beauty. Don't scratch the paint!" The door swings open and Beauty barrels into her. Anna buries her face in Beauty's fur and takes a deep breath. "Beauty, you are the best-smelling dog in the world!"

Inside, she sheds her pack and hides it behind the couch. "Good-bye, pack. Hello, snack." She feels suddenly free and light, as if she could float away. "Come on, girl."

She gets a package of Hostess Sno Balls out of the kitchen cupboard and unwraps it in front of the refrigerator. The three letters from Mica are posted on the door, held up by words out of the magnetic poetry set she gave Miss J for Christmas. The latest one is pinned in place with a poetic sentence she and Miss J came up with together:

the impervious dogs flicker and flounce

"School," she mutters, rereading Mica's GOOD NEWS! "You don't know what you're getting into."

She's peeling the rubbery skin off a Sno Ball when she notices two new magnetic sentences on the refrigerator door:

"They're coming over again?"

Beauty raises her good ear like a question mark. (Even the stub of the ear she lost in the car accident perks up.)

"You know who I mean. Mr. Webster and Trog."

Anna tears off a strip of icing and flips it. Beauty snaps it out of the air. "Big man for supper tonight. They were here two nights ago. You remember. Trog threw up on the kitchen floor. And Mr. Webster broke the chain on the porch swing—not that he meant to."

When the man and his dog are in the house, things just seem to break or fall on the floor, and Miss J gets so distracted that Anna feels invisible. Is it selfish to want Miss J all to herself? They have a lot of lost years to make up.

"Guess we'd better melt those eats," she tells Beauty.

As she slides the pan of frozen lasagna out of the freezer, she gets a little more worried. Miss J hates to cook, yet they spent a couple of hours of their Saturday stacking cheese and noodles. Miss J even called her mother for her special recipe.

The aluminum foil that covers the frozen lasagna turns misty with condensation. Anna finger-writes her name in curly letters. She thinks about how the letters will evaporate away, then erases them with her palm before that can happen.

"Come on, girl." Anna retreats to the backyard, Beauty at her heels. Side by side on the bench, they share the rest of Anna's snack. "Everything's okay. Really. I adopted you, Miss J will adopt me. It takes time." Anna picks up a stick off the ground and throws it. "Fetch, Beauty! Go get it, Smartest Dog in the World!"

But Beauty isn't a retriever.

She gets the part about chasing the stick, but when it lies motionless on the ground, she barks at it, then turns to Anna, like, here it is, come get it.

"Last time," Anna says when she gets tired of fetching her own stick. She throws it as hard as she can. The stick smacks the trunk of the Old Senator, then falls to the ground. Beauty dashes over to scold it—and that's when Anna sees a beautiful brown and white feather lying next to the stick.

"Good work, Beauty! Good find! We can send it to Mica." She goes inside and digs a pen and a sheet of notebook paper out of her pack. She slips the pen in her pocket and tucks the folded paper in the waist of her jeans.

Back outside, she sticks the owl feather behind her ear and climbs the ladder attached to the huge live oak. The paper inside her shirt scratches her stomach. Below, Beauty dances from paw to paw, barking.

She reaches the top of the ladder. "Come on up, girl! Come on!"

The dog cocks her head, whines.

"It's okay, girl. You wait there." Anna puts a sneaker on the limb the ladder is nailed to and steps up into the branches of the Old Senator. Steadying herself with a hand on the trunk, she concentrates on the big branch over her head. She stretches as high as she can, but nothing's changed since the last time. Even on tiptoes she can't get a good grip. She spits on her palms.

One deep breath…and…she jumps. Heart pounding, she hangs there, the bark cool against her palms. Before her fingers start to slip, she kicks her feet up as high as she can. The toe of her left sneaker catches on the branch—but it drags against the bark and slides off.

"Cripes!" She's hanging by her arms again. She could drop back down to the branch below, but she's on her way up, not down.

She kicks harder. This time she hooks her foot over the branch. Ignoring the pen jabbing her thigh, she wraps her legs around the limb and twists to the topside of the branch. As she pushes herself up with her arms, a breeze puffs her bangs back from her forehead. The bough sways. The next couple of branches up are easy. Anna sits on a nice wide limb up among the leaves.

At the foot of the tree, Beauty lies with her chin on her paws. "Up here, girl! Look up!" But dogs don't watch girls in trees—just squirrels.

Anna slides the paper out of her waistband and smooths it against the trunk. She takes the pen out of her pocket and writes, "Dear Mica."

She starts out with her rotten day at school, then wonders if she should cross it out. Mica's already scared about going to school. But who else can Anna talk to? She doesn't want to worry Miss J, who thinks that everything is fine. And maybe Mica needs to be warned.

She has just moved on to writing about the owl feather when she hears a shout. "Hey, Anna, hey! Down here!" She peers through the leaves. Ben's little brother Cody is hugging a ball to the chest of his striped T-shirt. "Cut that out," he sputters, balancing on the toes of his red high-tops to keep Beauty from licking him on the mouth. "No kissing!"

"What are you doing down there?"

"I was bouncing." He holds up the ball with both hands. "I saw you from the street. Can I come up too?"

Anna swings her legs. "I don't know. You're too little to come up here."

"Please? Your dog is licking me to death." He drops the ball in the grass and puts a foot on the ladder. "How about partway?"

"Okay. But be sure you stop partway."

When his feet are on the fifth rung, Anna warns, "High enough, Cody."

"Nuh-uh. Partway's higher than this."

"You sure?"

"Sure I'm sure." Cody keeps climbing.

"Stop at the top of the ladder!" Clenching the half-written letter in her teeth, Anna swings back down to the first branch. She crouches on the limb and reaches for him. "You can sit on the branch, but keep your feet on the ladder," she says, talking around the sheet of paper.

Cody ignores her hand. When he reaches the top rung he turns and sits on the branch. "Wow! Everything sure looks small from up here!"

Anna takes the letter out of her mouth and checks it for spit. She's smoothing out the tooth marks when she notices Cody is holding his thumb in front of his face, one eye closed. "What are you doing?"

He pulls the thumb closer. "Disappearing Beauty."

Anna bumps his thumb aside. "Don't *do* that!"

"Why not? I can't *really* make her disappear."

"It's just bad luck."

"Like it could make something really happen to her?"

Anna shrugs. "Maybe."

He kicks at the ladder. "I think I'll do it to Cass."

"You want something bad to happen to Cass?"

"No—I just want her to disappear." He turns toward Anna and his eyes narrow. "Why's that feather behind your ear?"

She shows him the tooth-dented paper. "I'm sending it to Mica in this letter. It's an owl feather."

"You know Mica?"

"Your brother gave me a letter from her. We're friends now. We send each other stuff."

"She's my friend too! My family almost adopted her."

"Really?"

"Well, kind of. My mom and dad wished they could bring her home with us when we left."

"Why?"

"I dunno. They didn't approve…"

"Of what?"

"Stuff… Can I write now?"

"What stuff?"

"Stuff about her dad." Cody reaches for the pen.

Anna hands it to him and presses the paper flat against his thigh. "Like what?"

"Shhh. I have to concentrate." He writes a giant *H* and a giant *I*. He sticks his tongue out of the corner of his mouth and keeps on writing. The pen pokes a hole in the paper. "Rats!" he says.

"That's okay. It gives the letter texture. What kind of stuff about her dad?"

"Hey, Anna. You know what?" He gives her back the pen. "Some owls nested in the tree in our backyard. They had two babies, but they kicked one out for being a grunt."

"You mean a 'runt'?"

"Yeah, a runt. I found him sitting in our birdbath. Miss J said to leave him alone 'cause it seemed like his parents were still feeding him. I named him Screeper."

"Did you really leave him alone?" Anna would have put the baby owl in a box and brought him in her room.

"I didn't *bother* him…" His eyes shift away. "I talked to him a lot," he admits.

"You probably kept him from being lonely."

"One day he flew away. Hey, maybe that's his feather." She lets him hold it but he quickly loses interest. "You want to kick my ball around?"

"Don't you usually do that with Ben?"

"Used to. Not anymore." He shuts one eye, holds up his thumb, and vanishes a cardinal in the crown of the tree. "Since we got back from the Keys he's *always* with Cass. It's like he turned stupid all of a sudden."

"Cass too." Of all the neighborhood kids, Cass was the nicest to her last summer. Even though she already had Jemmie Lewis as a best friend, it seemed then that she might have an opening for a second-best friend.

Then Cass started eighth grade. Then Ben happened.

Double whammy.

"Liking girls is really stupid." Cody glances over at her. "I mean mushy liking."

Anna remembers the pan of lasagna turning swampy on the counter. "Liking boys is stupid too. Hey," she says, brightening. Her foster mother's VW is pulling into the driveway. "There's Miss J!"

"And Mr. Webster," says Cody, pointing out the pickup right behind it. "He sure is here a lot. Is Miss J adopting him too?"

"You can't adopt a grown-up."

"You sure?"

Dear Mica,

I'm writing you from a really high branch in the Old Senator—as high as the top of your mast, I bet. Sorry if the ink looks bumpy. I'm using the tree trunk as my desk.

School was atrocious today. Ashlee again. We were in science class when a daddy longlegs walked between the desks. Ashlee screamed, "Ooooooh! A gross spider! Step on it!" I scooped it up in my hat. She told everyone I had a poisonous spider, so I told her daddy longlegs are not poisonous—they're not even true spiders, just close cousins. She said it didn't matter, they're creepy and ugly, which is just as bad.

Good thing she doesn't know I have a pet spider. I'm not sure where Charlotte is now that it's winter, but all summer we had to duck under her web to get to the door. Charlotte is a golden orb spider—I don't know the Latin name. I don't have the book up here. But she's big and beautiful with silver dots on her abdomen and hairy tufts on her many knees. She's so big that it's hard to notice her mate, a really small spider who hangs out at the edge of the web. He stays out of Charlotte's way and tries not to look like food.

Charlotte reminds me of Miss J. They're both big and right-out-there. Nothing scares either one of them. When I'm in school I act like Charlotte's mate. I stay out of the way and try not to look like food!

I hope things will be better for you at your new school. They have to be. No Ashlee.

When I'm up here I don't have to think about her. She would never climb a tree. She'd be too worried about scraping her hands or messing up her clothes or seeing a spider (or a close cousin).

Beauty found this feather in the grass under the Old Senator. It's from a barred owl. There aren't any owls in the tree at the moment. They swoop in at dusk.

HI FroM CoDY

Guess who just climbed the ladder? CoDY. He says to tell you that he used to have a pet baby owl named Screeper. We have to go play kickball now. C U later.

Anna

p.s. It's later. Mr. Webster (Miss J's friend) was here for dinner again. He's funny (tonight he was trying to show us a juggling trick and broke a plate), but he's big and his dog is big. When they're here our house feels too full. After they left Miss J said, "They're a handful and a half!" but she was smiling when she said it. While we were putting the dishes away (the ones that didn't break!), she asked me if I wanted to invite you to visit us this summer. That would make the house fuller, but in a good way. Can you come????

C U later-later.
Anna (your ss)

chapter 7

MICA TUGS AT HER SUDDENLY short hair, afraid the haircut Aunt
Emma's hairdresser gave her makes her look even younger. She
especially misses her long bangs. "What do you think? Do you
like it?"

"It's excellent." The Captain drops his spoon into his empty
bowl. "No one heats a can of stew as well as you."

"Not the stew, my hair!"

He has been in the presence of her hair throughout dinner
and hasn't said a thing about it. Now he cocks his head and
squints. "It's...cute."

Coming from her father, that might not be a compliment.
"Define cute."

"Cute, as in highly acceptable. You'll fit right in at school."

"But?"

"But...I don't know. You look different, more ordinary.
Before, you looked like yourself."

"Before, I looked tragic!" She cut her own hair the last time.
It was hard to reach the back, so it came out jagged.

"Not tragic. Unique." He picks up Anna's owl feather from
the table and sticks it behind her ear. "Better." But in a moment
he slides it back out. "Aunt Emma's probably right. It's time for

you to fit in." He reaches for the jacket that hangs on a hook by the sink.

"Don't go! Stay home, please," she begs. "It's my last night as a free person!"

"Don't be so dramatic. It's your bedtime anyway."

"Bedtime?" Her eyes widen. "I don't have a bedtime."

"Yes, you do. Nine thirty. Aunt Emma suggested it."

"Aunt Emma doesn't get a vote." She props her chin in her hands, dismissing the idea of bedtime. "Let's talk."

He slips his jacket on. "How about if I tuck you in before I go?"

"I'm too old to be tucked in."

"I suppose you are. I certainly did it plenty of times when you were younger, though."

He used to sit on the edge of her bed every night with a Peterson's field guide. "I remember. You quizzed me on birds."

"You got really good at them, even the warblers. They're always the hard ones." He snaps up his jacket.

"We could do that now..."

He starts for the ladder.

"Please stay, please."

"Come on, Mica. Be rational. I have to meet with Dr. Winn. Sharing a lab is proving to be difficult—you're a much better lab partner. His technique is sloppy, but we have to work it out. He thinks that in a friendly neutral setting—"

"Like a bar?"

"It's business, Mica. I can't do my work without lab space, and it's his lab. You'll be fine. The Floyds are close by if you need anything."

"Just stay 'til I fall asleep!" But she finds herself talking to his boots, the last thing to disappear through the hatch. The *Martina* lists as he climbs off. She doesn't hear anything for a minute; the Captain must be pushing the moped to the parking lot. Then the engine kicks on and the moped roars away.

She picks up Anna's feather and twists the shaft between her fingers. Doesn't he know it's her most important night ever? Can't he tell that she doesn't want to be alone? As soon as the sound of the motor fades, she slips off the *Martina* and pads down the dock to the houseboat. She peers through the window.

As usual, Uncle Bert is sound asleep in his lounge chair, mouth open. Aunt Emma is watching TV, a blanket across her lap. There's plenty of room on the sofa beside her, and the blanket would stretch, but Mica figures that if she knocks Aunt Emma will tell her it's past her bedtime.

Mica stands there for a while. Sometimes she watches Aunt Emma watch TV. When she gets tired of that she gazes across the inlet at Pirate's Bay Resort. It's a little dark to pick out the Captain and Dr. Winn at the waterfront bar. All she can see clearly are the strings of leftover Christmas lights reflecting in the water. The mosquitoes are biting her legs, so she gives up and goes home.

He's been gone thirty-two minutes by the galley clock—time enough to work things out with Dr. Winn. She listens for the buzz of the returning moped. All she hears is the fittings on the halyards clanging against the mast.

She lifts the curtain that shields her tiny cabin from the rest of the boat and crawls onto the narrow bunk where she sleeps. She pulls the crumpled sleeping bag over her knees. On the berth opposite, the one she doesn't use, is a pair of plaid shorts and a T-shirt. First-day-of-school clothes.

Mica opens the shallow cabinet by the porthole window and picks up the box that says "Leaping Lena—A proven salt water lure." Inside are three tree snail shells, each a little different. "You're going to Anna."

She tears a page out of her new notebook, selects a gel pen from the pack Aunt Emma bought for her, and starts a letter.

Dear Anna,

It's my last night before school and I'm alone on the boat. The Captain had to go out—so I'm pretending that you're here. You sure are quiet!

Okay—this is what I want you to do. Check out my clothes for tomorrow. Oops—if you're on the spare bunk you're sitting on them—not that it would make them worse. Move a little and take a look. What do you think? Are plaid shorts too weird??? The Captain wouldn't buy me new ones (he and Miss J are alike when it comes to clothes). Aunt Emma washed my T-shirts and shorts and picked out the ones she thought were good enough, which is not very many. Most of my clothes are too short or too tight or they have tar on them. Tomorrow I'm wearing the best of the worst.

Aunt Emma's hairdresser chopped my hair off. It stands straight up. I look like a chick getting its first feathers. And it definitely makes me look younger, which is bad. The Captain doesn't want me wasting time learning stuff I already know, so I'll be in eighth instead of sixth.

Here are some more shells. But these don't come out of the water. These snails (Liguus fasciatus) live in trees. (Do you think anyone at my new school knows about Latin names? If not, I can teach them.) Tree snails used to be more common in the Keys. They live in the hammocks (not the kind you lie around in)—small forests that grow in high spots on the islands. When hammocks are cut down to build houses, it's good-bye snails.

Uncle Bert says that some of the hammocks disappeared because of the snails. Snails can't travel far, so over time the snails evolved in these tree islands. Each group looked a little different. When a collector found a pattern he'd never seen before, he'd collect a couple—then burn down the hammock so no one else could ever find another specimen like his.

That was cheerful, wasn't it?

Your SS,
Mica

P.S. I hope school will be great. I'm tired of feeling like a one-of-a-kind tree snail.

P.P.S. Please send suggestions on how to look older. Realistic ones. The Captain suggested that I grow a beard. Ha. Ha.

P.P.P.S. We have golden orb spiders too. If Miss J is like the big female, the Captain is like the male, but only in size. He's small but he's tough! Tonight he told me I have a bedtime now. What's <u>that</u> all about?

Before heading for school the next morning, Mica stops in the marina office one last time. She's been in and out of the office a half dozen times already—mostly on hair-related missions. This time she presses the letter she wrote the night before into Aunt Emma's hand. "Can you mail this?" She fishes the "Leaping Lena" box out of the pocket of her shorts. "This too."

"Of course. Don't even think about it." Aunt Emma gives her a hug. "Good luck, honey. Today's your big day!"

"I hope!"

Aunt Emma holds up her crossed fingers. Mica returns the sign before running to the waiting moped.

She clings to the back of her father's jacket, wind filling the legs of her baggy shorts. The tires hum on the road, *school, school, school.* Mica feels the way she did the first time she dove off the mast. Scared and excited and tingly.

The Captain swerves into the Plantation Key School parking lot. While he props the bike on its kickstand, she notices the wire fence around the school. It looks like the pen she had in the Bahamas to hold land crabs. All the grass inside the fence is worn away. *Big land crabs,* she thinks.

She follows the Captain up a glaring white concrete walk. "After you." He holds the office door open for her. She wishes he'd go first.

Stepping inside, she inhales the school air. It smells stale, like it's been breathed way too many times. And there are hardly any windows—but maybe that's just the office. Mica plants herself in front of the counter. It would help if her father would say something, but his mind must be on last night's meeting with Dr. Winn. When he came home at eleven, she asked him how the meeting went. After a long pause he said, "A-de-quate-ly," making an effort to pronounce each syllable. "Are you sure you stuck to ginger ale?"

she asked. He only said it was way past her bedtime.

Mica tries clearing her throat, but the receptionist is printing a badge for a mother who is going to help someone named Miss Green with something called "student activity folders."

The receptionist finally looks up. "Yes? May I help you?"

Mica sees herself and the Captain reflected small in the woman's glasses. She waits for the Captain to speak. He's the parent. But only his body is there. His brain has left the room.

"I'm a new student," Mica watches her own tiny mouth say.

"Name?"

Her midget reflection stands straighter. "Mica Delano."

"Delano, Mica." The woman reads her name back to her off the tab of a file folder. She pulls a square of paper off the cover of the folder and holds it out to the Captain. "I have a sticky from our counselor. She says that although Mica's scores are high and she is academically qualified to enter eighth grade, sixth would be a much better fit for her socially." She raises her eyebrows at the Captain.

That wakes him up big-time. "Eighth grade is correct."

The receptionist runs a polished nail under the date of birth. "Perhaps seventh?"

"Eighth." The Captain taps the principal's signature on the bottom of the paper. The woman lifts her eyebrows even higher. The Captain ignores the eyebrows. "All set then?" he asks the receptionist. When she nods, he turns toward the door.

"Captain?" Mica grabs his arm.

"What? Oh. Yes, of course. Good luck. Have fun." He pats her head.

As he walks away her hand flies to her hair. She tries to feel whether or not any of it is sticking up funny. It was only lying down because Aunt Emma moussed it to within an inch of its life.

"Mica?" the woman at the desk calls. "Here are your schedule and map." Mica turns, still worried about her hair. She's taking the papers from the receptionist, relieved to see that her tiny head looks okay reflected in the woman's glasses, when she hears the door close. Her father is gone. Suddenly she feels very cold.

"To get to your homeroom you just go down the hall and turn left. Mrs. Bohannon's class is on the right. Room 24-A." The woman gives her a small chip of a smile, the kind that says, I'm too busy to give you a real one, but you get the idea. It's nothing like Aunt Emma's smile across the counter in the marina office.

Since no one is there when Mica walks into 24-A, she makes a logical choice of seats: Not in the very back; she *does* want to be noticed. But not at the very front either; she doesn't want to be *too* conspicuous. For seven and a half minutes she sits alone, surrounded by empty seats, alternately checking the door and the clock above the whiteboard.

She's making sure that Anna's feather is still inside her spiral notebook when the hall erupts. Two boys push into the room, falling through the door as if in this room gravity works sideways. The one who fell into the room first shoves the one behind him. "Thanks for the flat tire, jerk!" As he limps past her to a seat, Mica figures out what "flat tire" means: Boy A stepped on the back of boy B's shoe and made it come off. School language. She has a lot to learn.

Three more students tumble through the door, sucked in by the sideways gravity. They're girls, she's a girl. Mica waits for them to notice her. One of them turns slightly as she walks past. "Better get out of that chair if you don't want to get crushed. Big Farrell will be here any second."

She doesn't have a clue who Big Farrell is. This must be his chair. But if Big Farrell has a special chair, maybe *everyone* does.

The only way to *not* sit in someone's chair is to stand. She decides to stay put. Maybe Big Farrell is out sick today.

Mica tugs at her hair, sure now that it makes her look young for her age. On top of that, these kids are *not* her age. The way they look, act, and dress—everything is different about them.

Difference one: They all have packs. She has a pad, a handful of pencils, and a Flintstones lunchbox left over from one of Aunt Emma's sons.

Difference two: Every one of them has something denim on their lower half. Shorts, jeans. No plaid.

Difference three: What is going on under the girls' shirts? She doesn't believe her chest will *ever* look like that.

Difference four: Earrings. All the girls have them. Two of the boys do too.

She's checking out a boy with a diamond stud when a shadow falls across her desk, eclipsing the overhead lights. The giant girl who stands there opens and closes her mouth. "Uh…" She blinks stupidly. "You're in my place."

"Big Farrell?"

Except for her very pink cheeks, the girl's round face is the palest Mica has ever seen in the Keys. Her hair is white-blond, her eyelashes too—it's like the girl lives under a rock. Big Farrell shuffles a step closer, breathing loudly. "You're in my *assigned* seat." She acts like Mica's the one who's stupid.

"In a room full of seats, what makes one different from another? Why don't you sit in that one over there? Assigned seats are kind of pointless."

"Of course they're pointless. This is school." The girl's lips quiver. "But I *still* have to sit here."

"Okay, okay! Have your precious seat."

Hugging her school supplies and the hard metal lunchbox, Mica stands and steps away from Big Farrell's assigned seat. Now where's she supposed to sit? More students come in. Each one heads straight for a chair. They probably sit in the same spot every day—just like Aunt Emma on her stool.

A dark-haired woman—must be Mrs. Bohannon—walks in. Her eyes sweep the room. It doesn't take a second for the woman to see what is out of place. "Young lady?" She crooks a finger at Mica. "Are you sure you're in the right class, dear? Let me see your yellow paper."

She doesn't have a yellow paper, just a pink one and a white one, but she hands them over.

"No, dear, the *yellow* paper. This is your schedule and map."

"I know! But that's all they gave me in the office."

"Run to the office and tell them that Mrs. Bohannon needs the *yellow* paper."

Mica is running to the office when she spots the pair of double doors at the end of the hall. Those are the doors she and the Captain came in. Those are the doors to the parking lot, real air, wind, and sky. Daylight pours through them. She runs faster. She'll be back at the marina office by ten. Ha ha, big mistake, so sorry.

She's about to bump the push bar when a squeaky voice commands her to halt. Heart pounding, Mica whirls around. "No running in the hall!" It's just a kid with thick glasses, spiky hair, and a greenish yellow strap across his chest.

"But Mrs. Bohannon told me to run to the office."

"She didn't mean *run* run." The kid sounds disgusted. "She meant walk really fast. I'm going to have to write you up."

"Am I supposed to be scared?" she asks. "I don't care if you write me up."

As the kid blinks and sputters, the office door opens behind him. "Did Mrs. Bohannon send you to get this?" The receptionist holds out a yellow paper. "The bell's about to ring. Hurry now!"

"But don't run," says the kid wearing the strap.

Mica realizes a little late that she could outrun both the boy and the receptionist, but the woman rattles the yellow paper, so she trots up and takes it. As she speed walks toward homeroom, she wonders how the receptionist knew Mrs. Bohannon sent her when she only left the room a second ago. And what's with the weird little kid with the Day-Glo strap?

Then it hits her. School is an ant colony! Some scientists consider an ant colony a single organism. Connected by pheromone trails, ants are in constant communication. All members of the colony work toward the same goal.

The Day-Glo strap kid must be a guard ant, keeping *our* ants in and *their* ants out. She wants to tell him, I'm not one of *your* ants. I'm Mica Delano and I'm a whole different species.

Why didn't anyone warn her that Plantation Key School was a single organism that would try to assimilate her?

Her hand is on the knob of the classroom door when a buzzer blasts. As if they're one unit, all the ants in the room get to their feet and rush the door. They engulf her. The alarm must be a collective signal: Leave! Flee! Mica weaves through the swarm, waving the yellow paper over her head.

Big Farrell is the last to get to her feet. As she stands, one of the other ants knocks her purse on the floor. It's a huge, old-lady purse and everything inside it falls out.

"Did you see that?" Mica points toward Big Farrell, expecting the teacher to do something.

Mrs. Bohannon plucks the yellow paper out of Mica's hand. While she reads it, Mica holds the remaining papers and watches

Big Farrell crawl around, scooping pencils, cough drops, squished-up tissues, and three thick books back into her purse. Mrs. Bohannon acts like she doesn't know there's a really large pale girl crawling around on her floor.

Evidently satisfied with the yellow paper, the teacher lifts the white paper out of Mica's hand. "Let's see where you go next. Hmmm... Algebra in Portable One. The portables aren't on the map—someone needs to do a new one. The portables are right out back."

Big Farrell puts her palms on the edge of her assigned seat and hoists herself up. She looks upset as she huffs toward the door. "Colleen?" Mrs. Bohannon calls. But the girl doesn't even slow down. "Hurry and catch up to her," the teacher says. "She's going to algebra too."

Just as Mica reaches the door, a new group of students surges in. She butts her way through them. She doesn't want to lose sight of Big Colleen Farrell, who is chugging down the hall to the remote part of the ant colony known as Portable One.

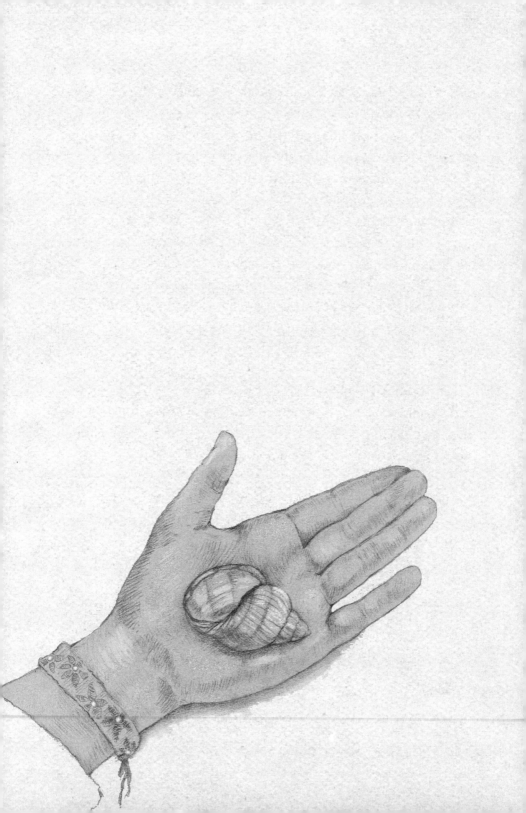

chapter 8

IT'S SATURDAY, AND ANNA IS cutting slabs of marble cake for their canoe trip. She feels so good she starts to hum. In a second Miss J is whistling along, adding a trilling harmony as she packs their sandwiches at the kitchen counter.

All week at school Anna has been hanging around with Ellen and Brianna—best friends since birth. All week, as the extra friend, Anna has been holding her breath.

When she woke up this morning, she finally let her breath out. Home for the weekend, she can ditch school-Anna and be herself. As soon as she and Miss J finish packing lunch, they'll tie the canoe to the roof of the VW and spend the day canoeing the Aucilla River, just the two of them. Humming and whistling, the notes go back and forth, answering each other. Anna feels as if they're carrying on a kind of conversation.

But Miss J stops in mid-whistle. "Hey, look. Mailman." Through the kitchen window they watch the truck pull up to the mailbox. "Go, Anna. It looks like a package!"

From Mica, please, Anna thinks, but she doesn't say it, afraid of jinxing things. She dashes down the walk. Smelling the exhaust from the mail truck, she sits on the curb and tears the package open. Inside is a box labeled "Leaping Lena," and inside that three shells carefully wrapped in a wad of tissues. Folded up under the shells are two sheets of lined paper, both covered with Mica's familiar handwriting.

Anna runs back to the house, eager to show Miss J, but when she reaches the kitchen a mayonnaisey knife lies on the counter. She can hear Miss J talking in the living room. She must be on the phone. That gives Anna time to read the letter.

The first thing Anna learns is that the shots and the paperwork must have been taken care of because, *ohmygosh, Mica's about to go to school.* Then Anna realizes that Mica wrote this last Sunday night. That means she's been in school for a whole week. Anna sincerely hopes school is going better for Mica than it is for her.

Anna feels bad that the Captain didn't even stick around on the eve of Mica's first day at school. Anna is luckier in the parent department. She has Miss J—which makes Anna realize she hasn't heard her foster mother's voice for a while. She sticks her head in the living room, but Miss J is gone and the phone is on the hook. Good. That means they'll go soon. Anna begins packing the cooler.

Miss J finally returns to the kitchen. Anna wonders why her hair looks more brushed—who needs brushed hair for canoeing?—but doesn't get to ask. "Hey," says Miss J. "A letter from Mica. What does she have to say?"

When Anna reads the part about the shell collectors burning trees so their specimens will be rarer, Miss J pounds her fist on the counter. "How did our stupid species get to be in charge of this beautiful planet?"

"We could put dogs in charge." Anna walks the box of snails to the living room and sets them on a shelf. By the time she gets back to the kitchen, Miss J has tossed two slices of bread on the counter and is making another sandwich—definitely one sandwich too many, but Miss J always gets distracted when she hears stories like that.

Anna fetches the paddles out of the broom closet. "Want to put the canoe on the car?"

"Shoot! I forgot to mention that was Jonah on the phone."

"Is he canoeing with us?" *Not a good plan,* Anna thinks, *given the smallness of our canoe and the largeness of Mr. Webster.* "He might sink us."

"He would, wouldn't he? But he won't get to sink us. There's been a change of plans. Would you mind getting me the mustard?"

When Anna delivers the mustard she smells perfume—definitely not an everyday Miss J smell. "What's the new plan?"

Her foster mother twists the lid off the mustard jar. "He says they just cut a new road through the national forest. The plow always turns up fossils and pottery. We're going to check it out. Fun, right?" Miss J dips a knife in the mustard and stops. "You're okay with this, aren't you?"

"Are you sure you want me along? I could stay here and do homework."

"You don't have any homework, remember? You don't have any, I don't have any. We did the chicken dance of joy about it last night."

They had performed their wonky celebration dance, tucking their thumbs under their armpits and flapping bent wings—but that was before Mr. Webster called. "I could watch TV or something while you go on your date. It's okay."

"Date, schmate. This is a field trip." Miss J's hands are full, but she leans over and kisses Anna's shoulder. "This is *our* day. Yours and mine. Jonah and Trog are just tagging along—we'll let them carry our stuff."

Remembering the way she felt tagging along after Ellen and Brianna, she almost feels sorry for the man and his dog.

Miss J picks up the floppy stack of ham, cheese, bread, and assorted condiments. "Help me wrestle this into a Baggie."

Anna opens the plastic bag as wide as it will go. "What did you put on this thing, anyway?"

"Everything. The man has a healthy appetite."

There's a loud knock on the door. Miss J jumps. A slice of ham falls out of the sandwich and lands on the floor. Normally Miss J would pick it up, wash it off, and stuff it back in the sandwich—Anna's foster mom hates to waste anything—but today she's distracted.

Beauty lunges out from under the table and inhales the ham.

"Could you get the door while I wash the ham grease off my hands?"

Anna walks slowly across the living room. On the other side of the door are the inevitable Mr. Webster and his inescapable dog Trog. But they can wait a few more seconds. She stops to look at the scarab beetles sitting in a neat row on their shelf. They remind her of the water bugs that zip ahead of the canoe and shine like silver nail heads in the sunlight. Anna hasn't quite let go of the day they'd planned on the river.

Another knock on the door. She pretends it's a pileated woodpecker hammering a nest hole in an oak on the bank.

"Anna?" Miss J calls from the kitchen. "Did you drink slow juice for breakfast?"

Anna crosses the room and turns the knob of the purple door. It's barely clicked when Mr. Webster bursts in like a strong wind, Trog right behind him. "Oh, Anna. Hi."

Is he surprised to see her? Maybe he thought she'd be somewhere else, doing something with friends. She wants to remind him it's *her* day, hers and Miss J's. "Hi, Mr. Webster."

"*Mr. Webster?* He glances over his shoulder. "Is my dad around here somewhere?"

"I…I mean, Mr. Jonah?"

"How about just Jonah? Or…or…what about Science Guy?" He stuffs his hands in his pockets. "I kind of like Science Guy."

Tails stiff, Trog and Beauty circle each other, sniffing butts. The fur on Beauty's back is rucked up; her tail quivers. That's Beauty's suspicious wag. The dogs aren't doing much better than the humans when it comes to greeting each other.

Mr. Webster jangles the change in his pockets and shifts his weight from one foot to the other. "So…good week at school?"

"Pretty good."

He nods as if this is serious business, then cracks a smile. "That was a dumb question, wasn't it? The kind adults always ask kids."

"That's okay. You're an adult."

"Well then…how's your left foot?"

Anna blinks up at him. "My what?"

"Gotcha!" he says, pointing. "Didn't expect that one from a grown-up, did you?"

She looks down at her feet. "My left foot is fine, thank you. The right one too." When she glances back up he looks uncertain. He can't tell that she's kidding. She keeps her face straight. "Are you sure you're a grown-up?"

"In size only."

"What about the beard?"

He runs a hand over his shaggy brown beard. "Oh, that. I've had it since I was nine."

Anna can't hold back a little smile. He's not so bad. She only wishes she could tell him to come back later—like a couple of years from now. If she and Miss J had had some time to themselves first, having Mr. Webster around might be okay. He could ask his dumb-funny questions. Miss J could wear perfume for him. But Miss J met Mr. Webster right about the time that Anna moved in with her. Anna wishes she'd had a head start.

"Show him the snails Mica sent," Miss J calls from the kitchen.

Anna retrieves the fishing lure box and opens the lid.

He hunches over, peering into the wad of tissue. "Tree snails," he declares.

"*Liguus fasciatus.*"

"Hey, we'll have to call *you* Science Guy."

"It was in Mica's letter." She tells him about the collectors burning down the hammocks.

"That's pretty bad," he says. "But I'll tell you a worse one. There was an ornithologist who wanted some great auks to stuff for his collection. He knew they were getting scarce and he didn't want to miss out, so he hired a couple of fishermen to club as many as they could and bring them back. They got two, but that was all they could find. Thanks to that ornithologist, the great auk had just become extinct."

"You read that in *A Treasury of Birdlore!*" Miss J is standing in the door. "I kept that book by my bed when I was a girl!"

Mr. Webster smiles over Anna's head. "Hey, me too!"

"You used be a girl?" Anna jokes, but no one's listening.

With long strides Mr. Webster crosses the distance between him and Miss J.

"Come in here, you two," says Miss J, dodging a hug. "Choose your junk food for the trip."

Following slowly, Anna feels like the visitor. By the time she gets to the kitchen, Trog is licking the spot on the floor where the ham fell, as if Beauty hadn't done a good enough job. Even Science Guy's dog has a take-over personality.

Mr. Webster is hugging a bag of ranch-flavored chips. He leans down and snuffs at Miss J's neck. "Nice perfume," he growls. Having Mr. Webster around is like owning a pet bear.

Miss J shoos him away, but she's blushing and smiling. "What do you say we hit the road?" She distributes the snacks between a couple of backpacks and slides her arms through the straps of one of them. Mr. Webster takes the other. They each grab a handle on the cooler. The only thing Anna carries is her uncle's hat.

The dogs spring into the back of Mr. Webster's pickup. Anna wishes she could ride with them. The truck cab is really crowded. With Mr. Webster driving, Miss J in the passenger seat, and her in the middle, she feels like a skinny slice of baloney in a great big bun.

Mr. Webster's arm drapes the back of the seat, his fingers on Miss J's shoulder. As daylight flickers through the trees of the Apalachicola National Forest, Mr. Webster whistles a tune Anna's never heard. In a second Miss J is whistling along, the two of them having a conversation she can't join.

Anna is lying on her bed, her muddy sneakers kicked off on the floor. She listens to Miss J and Mr. Webster laugh in the next room. Anna excused herself and said she had homework. Miss J knew she didn't have any. Or used to know. But with Mr. Webster in the house she's forgotten all about the chicken dance of joy and the plans they had for a weekend without homework, a weekend of doing whatever they wanted to do together.

Anna thinks about Mica the night before the start of school, alone on the boat. Miss J would never let her down like that. Today is just an ordinary Saturday. They'll have lots of Saturdays to float down the river. Lots and lots. And with President's Day on Monday, they still have two possible days to canoe this weekend.

But when another peal of laughter comes from the living room, Anna lets her mind drift down to the Keys, and she imagines she is aboard the *Martina* with Mica, sitting on Mica's extra bunk—she can almost feel the motion of the boat. When the sound of Mr. Webster and Miss J having a good time doesn't go away, she opens her eyes and reaches for her notebook.

Dear Mica,

Isn't it weird? You're a year younger than me but you'll be a year ahead. It won't be easy. You'll be fine, though. You're advanced when it comes to school. Not me. Every time I change schools, they're teaching something different. Sometimes I'm ahead and sometimes I'm behind. I went from a school that hadn't started cursive to one where they all knew how. I had to figure out how to attach the letters to each other by myself. I got multiplying fractions three times.

Just remember, the first few days of school are the worst. Trust me. I'm an expert at being new.

The story about the tree snails reminds me of the woods that used to be in our neighborhood. One day we found out they were going to bulldoze them. We got everyone together—even Ben and Cody—and we dug up little trees and ferns and bushes. We planted them all over the neighborhood. If you were here, I'd walk you around and show you. But even though we watered them for weeks, there aren't too many survivors. We did our best but we only saved a few plants, which isn't the same as a woods. A woods is everything all together.

Trying to save the woods is how we met Mr. Webster. Miss J called the County Office of Environmental Management, and he answered the phone. He's an environmental planner. Even though he couldn't stop the bulldozers, he helped us dig up plants. Since then he's always around our house. Miss J says they're not dating, but I think they are—if you can call it a date when you bring a kid (me) along.

What I'm sending you is from their latest not-date. These are shards of Paleo-Indian pottery. "Paleo" means they're really, really old. We found them when we were walking along a new road through the national forest. When the sand got turned, the pottery showed up. The oldest pieces are about two thousand years old. The Indians who made them are extinct—like those tree snails in the burned-down hammocks—or if they are here at all, they live just like the rest of us now. I found most of the shards. Even the dogs found more than Miss J and Mr. Webster. They were too busy talking and looking at each other.

Your SS,
Anna

p.s. I forgot to answer your question about how to look older. Maybe you should wear tall shoes. (It's better than your dad's advice to grow a beard.) I have the same problem. Even though I'm the right age I look young. I could pass for a fourth grader. Seriously.

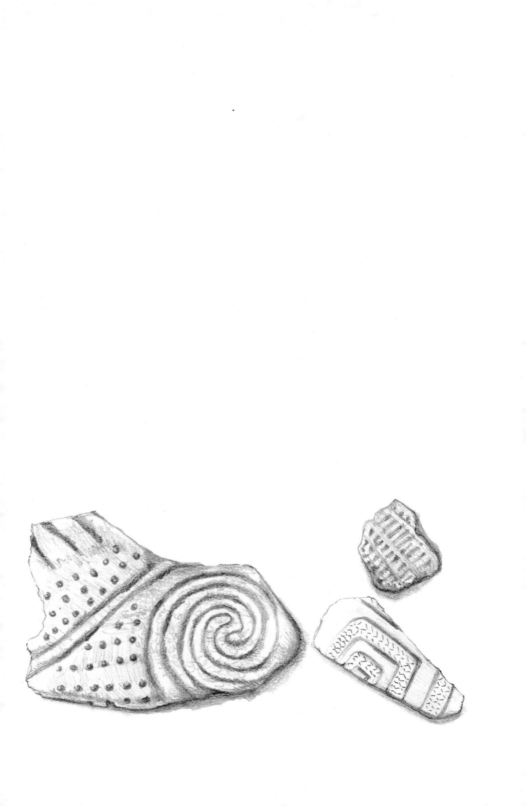

chapter 9

"MICA?" THE CAPTAIN PULLS BACK the curtain, and the light of another school day slaps her in the face. "Mica, get up. You're going to be late."

"I'm sick," she croaks, pulling the edge of the sleeping bag over her head.

"Sick? You mean sick of school." He pulls the zipper down and flips the top of the bag aside. "Come on. It's Friday. You had Monday off, so it's been a short week. Surely you can last one more day."

Mica curls up like a cooked shrimp. "I can't! I'm sick. *Real* sick." She keeps her eyes shut, hoping he'll go away.

"Symptoms?" he demands.

"My throat hurts…and I threw up during the night…" He can't say she didn't. He was out pretty late.

She feels his hand on her forehead. Luckily she's warm from being in bed and his hand is cold. And it's also lucky for her that he's too worried about his work with Dr. Winn to have the energy to make her go to school. "I'll tell Aunt Emma to come check on you later," he says. While he downs another cup of coffee she pretends to be asleep.

But as soon as he leaves she opens her eyes. Staring at the white headliner over the bunk, she listens until the sound of the moped's engine thins and disappears. She sits up. "Yes!" she shouts. "Yes!"

She wriggles into her swimsuit—her second skin until school made her shed it. She covers the suit with a pair of shorts that are too old and comfortable for school. She doesn't brush her hair.

When she goes up on deck she fills her lungs with fresh, salty air. The dragonflies resting on the ropes that droop between the stanchions sparkle like jewels. She kneels down next to one and stares at its compound eyes and wonders what it would be like to see the world as dozens of tiny images instead of one big picture.

She goes inside just long enough to grab a couple of bread slices. Back on deck she tears off a piece of crust. Before tossing it in the air she makes sure there are no gulls in sight—that's part of the game. Then, staring up at the blank blue sky, she flings it as high as she can. She immediately hears wings and a piercing cry. "Hello, *Larus atricilla!*" she yells at the laughing gull that appears out of nowhere. "Did ya miss me?"

Toss anything in the air, even a pebble, and a gull will materialize. If the flying object is remotely edible, the gull will scarf it down. Sometimes they'll even eat the pebble. By the time Mica tosses the last piece of bread, the sky above the *Martina* is crowded with circling, arguing gulls. She's reassured. Everything in the *real* world works just the way it did before she started school.

She stretches her arms out to feel the sun. How could she have ever taken the sun for granted? At PKS the sun is replaced by tubes that buzz like trapped flies. They turn everything a dusty blue. The views out the windows—and there aren't many windows—feature the parking lot, dead grass, the fence, a pair of Dumpsters, the portables, and the rack of chained bicycles.

The wind riffles her short, school-cut hair and she remembers the Captain's word: ordinary. School is making her ordinary. "Not!" she shouts at the sky. "I'd like to see someone ordinary do this!" She shimmies up the mast and stands on the spreader. The gentle motion of the sailboat is amplified up the length of the mast. The mast swings back and forth and she rides it.

Ben Floyd dove off the mast, but not until the last day of his vacation. It wasn't even a real dive. He jumped feet first. *Bet he still brags about it,* she thinks. She made fun of him, but now she knows, for a guy usually locked up all day in school he did all right.

The sun glints on the chain around her neck—she forgot to take it off. A few days in school, and she's already starting to unlearn the natural world. She always warns tourists: "Don't wear shiny things in the water unless you want to attract barracudas." She fingers her mother's ring. It is the goldest and shiniest thing on the chain, the most likely object to lure a barracuda. But on the chain with it are more attractors: the key to the shower room and the silver dolphin charm she, Ben, and Cody found in a sunken toolbox they brought up from the bottom.

The Captain says there's no such thing as luck, but Mica likes to think the charm is lucky. She tucks all three shiny objects into the top of her suit and somersaults off the mast. From that height she plunges deep, down to the lightless depths where the water girl hides.

When she comes up, Mica feels sure that the ordinariness of school has been washed out of her. Tonight she'll call a meeting of the board to announce that she isn't going back to PKS. Didn't the Captain say that when it comes to school she has the deciding vote?

She's swimming like a gator, just her eyes above the water, when she hears her Zodiac chafing at the stern of the *Martina*, urging her to climb aboard and motor down Snake Creek.

Maybe she wasn't completely faking when she told the Captain she was sick. In the sunlight her skin does look pasty and pale. School has turned her the color of chalk dust and she needs to get her real color back. Besides, sun on your skin makes vitamin D. Sunlight is a kind of medicine—the exact kind of medicine she needs.

Mica ducks back into the galley just long enough to grab a Pop-Tart.

Pop-Tart in hand, she hops down into the Zodiac. She doesn't notice Aunt Emma, who is carrying a package from Anna down the dock to the sick girl aboard the *Martina*. Mica pull-starts the motor and heads for Snake Creek.

The meeting of the board isn't going the way Mica planned. "Aunt Emma busted me?"

"You said you were sick. She offered to keep an eye on you and you skipped out. It was her duty to tell me."

"I skipped out because I hate school, Captain. I tried it and I hate it and I'm not going back!"

"The grant isn't exactly fun, either." Her father folds his hands on the dinette table. "But you and I have been bouncing from one thing to another for far too long. We need to persist."

"But it's pointless! I move that Mica Delano be allowed to go back to homeschooling."

The Captain rubs his eyes. "Motion denied. We need to play it straight for a change. We've been running away from things for too long."

"But I have the deciding vote!"

"Not anymore. Aunt Emma says a family is not a democracy."

Dear Anna,

I loathe and despise school! I gave it a chance. I went a whole week and a half, so I know for sure. I would rather suck down a box of rotten bait than go back. The kids at school are a whole different species. <u>Homo stupidus.</u> And every one of them has a friend or two grafted to them.

School is for lower life forms. Bells ring and everyone swarms to their next class. The office gave me a dinky map. Half the classrooms weren't even on it. After homeroom, which was just down the hall from the office, I was the last one to get to every class. Whenever I walked into a room, the kids all turned like a school of fish and stared at me.

In science class we're studying photosynthesis. Duh... Who doesn't know about that? The teacher (her name is Ms. Groark, like a frog mating call) asked a question. The girl she called on obviously didn't have a clue, but she kept staring down like the answer was going to appear on her desktop. I guess we were supposed to sit there and wait for her to grow a brain. Finally I just yelled out the answer—stoma! Ms. Frog told the class that I was homeschooled and that I didn't know about good classroom manners. Then she told me to raise my hand and wait to be called on. Classroom manners are for lower life forms (like slime molds).

I flunked lunch the first day. I finished eating and went outside. Big crime! I didn't wait for the lunch person to march us out (if these kids don't know the way by now someone should drown them).

I didn't get caught leaving. I guess everyone thought I was some younger kid who wandered into second lunch. First lunch was still on the playground when I got there. I had to knock two boys down to break up a game of lizard stomp. I met the principal. She agreed that stomping lizards is gross but liked it better than me punching fourth graders. Here's what she said to do in the future: I tell a teacher, the teacher tells her, and then she handles it. By then the lizard would be a splat on the pavement. That was okay with her as long as I follow the rules. Did I mention that I HATE school???

Today I told the Captain that I was sick. He let me stay home, but Aunt Emma ratted me out when she saw me take off in my Zodiac! She said that she had to because school is an obligation. That's way different from what she said when she came up with the idea for me to go in the first place. Then it was all about fun! And making friends—like _that_ worked out. Plus I _was_ sick (school-sick) and the best cure was to take my Zodiac deep into the mangrove tunnels along Snake Creek and imagine that school is in some distant galaxy a million zillion light years away.

I'm in my V-berth in the bow. The curtain is down, but I wish I had a real door because I can hear the Captain loud and clear. He's lecturing me about how you have to finish what you start and live with your decisions. I usually hate it when he goes out at night. Right now I wish he would.

Thanks for the pottery pieces. I don't have anything in here to send you, and I'm not going into the galley where the Captain is going on and on about my tragedy. But I'm still sending you something. Look closely at the piece of tape (ignore the fingerprints) and you will see there's an eyelash stuck to it. Mine. I think I'll mail myself to you one piece at a time. Ben can help you put me back together. He can't swim, but he's mechanical.

Your SS—me

chapter 10

THEY'RE EATING BREAKFAST WHEN Miss J says, "Hey, I almost forgot!" and dashes into the living room. Anna hears her bumping around, then she's back. "Surprise!" Miss J looks at her hopefully, a shoe dangling from each hand. "I picked 'em up at Goodwill on my way home from work. You like them? They're so sturdy and they're almost new."

"They do look sturdy." Anna twists the bottom edge of her cousin's sweater.

"You can't wear sneakers all the time, can you? And it's definitely too cold for those old sandals of yours. I don't want you to get sick."

Anna eyes the shoes. Brown, with chunky heels, big buckles, and square toes—they look like something Ben Franklin would have worn.

Miss J sets them on the kitchen floor, heels facing Anna. "Want to try 'em? They're your size."

Using the toe of her left foot, Anna pries her old sneaker off her right foot. She squiggles her toes into the shoe. Maybe, just maybe, it won't fit.

"Well, look at you!" Miss J claps her hands together. "It fits like Cinderella's slipper. Try the other one." Anna puts on the other shoe. "Okay now, walk around. Take those puppies for a test drive."

Anna clomps around the kitchen. The heels are thicker than she's used to and they make a lot of noise.

"You like them? They look good to me, but what do I know? I'm not much of a role model in the femininity department." She lifts her own foot, displaying the usual worn army boot and purple sock. "Purple socks are as feminine as I get. So, what do you think?"

For a second she sees the shoes the way Miss J does. Practical. Sturdy. Stamped on the sole are the words ALL MANMADE MATERIALS, so nothing died for her feet.

But then school-Anna reminds her, *you'll be wearing them in front of Ashlee.*

If only they weren't so practical and sturdy. If only they weren't so brown. But Miss J has that little knot between her eyebrows that means she's worried, so Anna says, "I like them. Thank you."

"You are highly welcome!" As her foster mom's eyebrows relax, Anna realizes that when it comes to being a mom, Miss J lacks confidence. If Anna has to wear Ben Franklin's shoes to school to reassure her, it's worth it.

Anna thumps over to the sofa and drags her backpack out from behind it. She stuffs in her sneakers for PE.

Knowing Miss J is watching her and the brown shoes, Anna tromps to the end of the path, then turns back and waves.

She's just decided that the shoes aren't that bad—they fit and they don't hurt—when Cass calls to her. "Hi, Anna!"

As Anna waits for the group to catch up, she notices the way Cass's eyes skim down to the shoes, then veer away.

"Some shoes," Leroy hoots. "You get them from your granny?"

"Hush!" Jemmie knuckles him in the shoulder. "She doesn't have a granny."

"Then she must've knocked over someone else's granny, 'cause *those* are granny shoes."

"I didn't choose them," Anna says, watching the gold buckles flash as she walks.

"Miss J did?" Cass asks.

"Yes." But she stops there. Making a comment about Miss J would be disloyal. Switching to her sneakers would be disloyal too—although she is definitely tempted. But suddenly she feels stubborn. After all, they're just a pair of shoes, so what's the big deal? Too bad they clomp as she walks, calling attention to themselves.

They reach the school just as bus 29 pulls up. Anna knows that's Ashlee's bus. She can see the girl's blond hair through the front window. Ashlee appears at the bus door just as Anna clomps past.

Ashlee stops at the top of the bus steps.

She stares.

"Attention, Goodwill shoppers!" Ashlee announces. "Today's special is ugly shoes on aisle nine."

"Just keep walking," Cass whispers, sliding her arm through Anna's and tugging on it.

But Anna stops. The rubber soles of her practical shoes grip the pavement. Cass can't budge her. Anna stares at Ashlee. "Why are you so mean?" she asks. "They're just shoes!"

"Good for you," Cass whispers, squeezing her arm as she leads Anna away.

When Anna looks back over her shoulder, Jemmie is standing in her place, knuckles on her hips. With Jemmie's gaze on her, Ashlee looks like one of Miss J's pinned bugs. "You heard Anna," Jemmie says. "Get over yourself, girl."

Dear Mica,

I thought about sending you a snip of hair (seemed like a good trade for the eyelash) but since Miss J gave me a haircut I don't have any to spare. Adults should never be allowed to play with scissors.

Instead I'm sending you this shell from an Eastern box turtle (<u>Terrapine carolina</u>) that we found in the woods. The bottom shell (the plastron) is in two pieces. That's because the muscle that used to hold it together is gone now—along with the turtle. I guess that their get-out-of-trouble strategy of pulling their legs and heads inside and closing up tight doesn't always work. Still, some days at school I wish I had a shell that closed up that tight.

But I don't and you don't, so here's my best fitting-in advice (from my vast store of new-kid-at-school knowledge):

1. Don't act too smart.

2. Don't act too dumb.

3. Don't eat anything at lunch that can get stuck in your teeth.

4. To find a friend fast, look around for a leftover person—someone no one is hanging out with—and talk to them. There's always a reason no one likes them, but it's usually stupid. In my last school I had a friend named Esther. One of her legs was shorter than the other. She had to wear one thick shoe. Everyone stayed away from her. All they saw was her thick shoe, but that was just one thing about her.

Miss J told me about an experiment where they painted a bird a different color and the flock drove it away. To them the bird wasn't one of them anymore. Miss J didn't know if they got the paint off after the experiment. I hope they did.

If you want a friend, find the kid with the different paint.

Bye 4 now,
Your Sorta Sister Anna

p.s. I tried to figure out how much it would cost to mail a person—more than a thousand dollars and every square inch would be covered with stamps. You could fly here cheaper—and it wouldn't be so messy. Miss J says you can visit anytime. Come, and we'll be different together.

a box in a box !

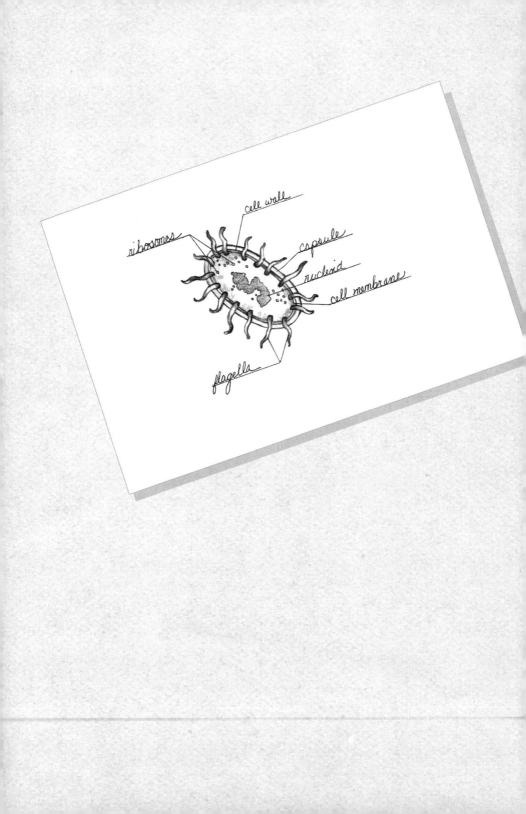

chapter 11

MICA HAS BEEN FOLLOWING Big Colleen Farrell for more than three weeks; they're in all the same classes. Mica knows the way by now, but in a crowded hall it's easier to skim along behind Colleen like a dinghy being towed by a bigger boat.

Sometimes she catches Colleen looking at her out of eyes half hidden behind white eyelashes. A couple of days ago when they were both at the water fountain, they almost talked. Then Colleen pushed the button too hard and the water slurped down the front of her shirt. Mica knelt to retie her sneaker and pretended not to notice. When she looked up, Colleen was plowing through the kids ahead of her, making her escape down the hall.

That's as close as Mica has come to talking to anyone at the school who isn't a teacher.

It's not like she hasn't tried to fit in. At first she tried to impress everyone by showing how smart she was, but Anna's right. No one likes you if you wave your hand around and volunteer correct answers all the time. She heard Ryan Smith call her a know-it-all. It should be a compliment, but it isn't.

When being right all the time didn't gain her any friends, she tried answering wrong. That didn't work either. She doesn't wave her arm around anymore, but if a teacher calls on her, she gives the right answer. Why look dumb for these dummies?

Big Colleen never raises her hand either. When she's called

on, she strangles on the words as if she's inhaled them and has to choke them back out. But her answer is always right too. It's the halting way she says the answer that makes it sound wrong.

Still, Mica has figured something out: Inside that big, stumbling body, there's a brain. It seems like she and Big Colleen are the only ones around here who know how to think, the only ones who haven't been assimilated by the ant colony.

After a morning of not raising their hands while other kids groped toward answers as obvious as eels' teeth, Mica and Big Colleen stand in the lunch line. Aside from the food—which Mica thinks is great—lunch is the worst time of day for both of them. They always fill their trays and then head in different directions, each of them claiming a seat at the empty end of an otherwise crowded table. Today will be no different. Mica will eat alone, pretending she doesn't notice the kids trading desserts, the girls with their heads together as if what they have to say is secret and important. She'll keep her eyes on her plate or study the second-grade art displayed on a distant wall. Every time she sneaks a glance at Colleen, her classmate will be staring into her own lap, reading. No book could be that interesting.

Mica gives her tray a shove and thinks back to the stupid science class she just sat through. "Imagine not knowing prokaryotic," she grumbles.

"An organism such as a bacteria or virus or algae that lacks a true nucleus," Big Colleen says, not looking at her. "Like, duh…"

Mica is shocked. Not because Colleen knows the answer— she and Colleen were the only ones who got it right on the science test. She's shocked because Colleen is talking! Mica stares at the back of the girl's head. *Talk to me,* she thinks. *Come on, talk.*

Mica waits, but Colleen pushes her tray along, mute as a rock.

As Mica predicted, today's lunch will be a repeat of every

other lunch. She's about to console herself with school ravioli—it's way more homemade than the canned kind she heats for the Captain—when Colleen speaks again.

"That's *pro*karyotic." Colleen is still facing away. "What I want to know is this: What is *anti*karyotic?"

"Anti?" says Mica. "Anti means against. So if you are *anti*kariotic you must dislike organisms that lack a true nucleus."

"Are you pro?" Colleen asks, taking a quick glance at Mica. "Or anti?"

"Pro...I guess." Mica hopes that's the right answer. "You?"

"Definitely pro."

They've reached the hot food part of the line. The woman behind the counter who always smiles at Colleen ladles up a huge serving of gooey red ravioli and plops it on a plate. "Here you go." She passes the plate to Colleen with a smile. Mica has noticed that she loads Colleen down every day. This lunchroom lady makes Big Colleen look like a tadpole. Her arms are cushioned with fat, although her hands look tiny like a doll's. When she smiles at Mica, too, Mica notices that she has a nice face and shiny auburn hair under her hairnet. "Ravioli?" the lunch lady asks.

"Yes, please." The woman is dipping up a regular portion when Colleen nods toward Mica. The woman gives her a megadose too. "You want to sit together?" Mica blurts out as she hands her money to the cashier.

"Sure," says Big Colleen, then she stalls out. "Where?"

Mica guides her to the spot where she usually eats alone, staring at the wall. But this time there will be two of them sitting together at the end of the table—talking, hopefully. Before Colleen can open the book on her tray, Mica says the first thing that comes into her head. "That woman sure is nice to you."

"She has to be. She's my mom."

Dear Anna,

I found the bird with the different paint! Her name is Colleen Farrell and she's in all my classes. She's smart. (She skipped a grade too.)

Her mother's name is also Colleen Farrell and she works in the cafeteria. The kids call them Big Farrell and Bigger Farrell or just Big and Bigger. Colleen's size is like your friend Esther's thick shoe. People make a big deal out of the most unimportant things.

Colleen and I have decided to eat together every day and walk to class too. She'll probably come over to the boat. or I'll go to her house. We formed a club called the Club of 2. To make it official we wrote the number 2 on the back of each of our left hands. It wasn't long before someone broke down and actually talked to us! At lunch Stephanie Paige asked what the 2 meant. We wouldn't tell. She guessed things like "2 fat" and "2 dorky" and even "2-na." The more she guessed, the more we kept our mouths shut. Finally she gave up and went back to not talking to us. We didn't care.

Colleen and I agreed you can write a 2 on your hand if you want. But don't forget. To be a member you have to be prokaryotic. Ha ha.

What I'm sending you is a drift seed. Aunt Emma dipped it out of the basin with the shrimp net. I don't know the Latin name or even what plant would grow out of it. The Captain doesn't either. Botany is not his specialty. I'll tell you everything Aunt Emma knows about it—which is basically nothing. She's <u>really</u> not a botanist. She calls it a Hamburger Hot Bean. Hamburger, because it looks like one. Hot Bean, because if you rub it on a rug it gets really hot.

Gotta go do homework now. So bye.

Mica

P.S. Thanks for the painted bird advice. It worked!

chapter 12

WHEN ANNA GETS HOME FROM SCHOOL, Cody is sitting on the step in front of the purple door, jiggling his knees. "Ben and Cass walked by a gajillion minutes ago. What took *you* so long? "

"A gajillion minutes? Really?" Anna had let the others get ahead, but she never lost sight of them.

"Okay. Maybe only half a gajillion," he admits. Since the day they climbed the tree he's come over a lot. Ashlee would think it's pathetic. A seventh-grade girl hanging out with a little boy. But when Cody grins up at her, showing off the two stubby teeth just coming in at the front of his mouth, Anna makes a decision: Everything that happens inside the stone wall is her own business, not Ashlee's or anyone at school's. None of *them* ever call her, or invite her over to their houses. None of them would wait for her on her doorstep for half a gajillion minutes.

As she hooks the key-string around her neck, Cody scrambles to his feet. "Hey. Wanna see what I found? It's for Mica." And he digs a tin box out of his pocket.

When Anna swings the door open, Beauty, who's been whimpering inside, lunges tongue-first at Cody. The tin box flies out of his hand and skitters across the floor. "Oh no, oh no, you bad dog!" Cody crawls after the box. "Bet you prob'ly broke it!"

"The box looks fine, Cody. And she's *not* a bad dog."

The metal lid opens with a rusty squeak. "Look what you went and did!" he yells at Beauty. "Broke off a leg!"

Inside the box, cradled in a nest of tissue, is an ox beetle. Half a dozen just like it (except with six attached legs) sit on the shelf in the bookcase along with other scarabs and a few click beetles, part of Miss J's collection, but it was nice of Cody to bring it over. "An ox beetle is a great thing to send Mica. And don't worry, Cody. We can glue it." She looks up from the shiny black beetle. "You didn't kill it, did you?"

"It was dead when I found it."

"You sure?"

"*Way* dead." He rolls his eyes. "Ants were dragging it!"

They go to the kitchen to perform what Cody calls "dead bug surgery."

Anna takes a tube of superglue and a box of toothpicks out of a drawer. "You have to be careful with this stuff," she warns, fishing a scrap of cardboard out of the recycling bin. "Anything that gets glued with it stays stuck forever. So don't touch it." She squirts a thin stream onto the cardboard and gets out a toothpick. Then she takes the magnifying visor that hangs on the gooseneck lamp by the sofa and puts it on. The band that holds it on slides down until it rests on top of her ears. She peers at Cody through the lenses.

"Alien, alien!" Cody chants. But the chant changes to "let me, let me" when she selects a pair of tweezers from the dissecting kit Miss J keeps in the silverware drawer. "Let me glue it! I found the beetle." He puts his face so close to hers that his eyes are huge in the magnifying lenses.

"No, I'd better," says Anna. "I've done it before." Using the toothpick, she dips up the tiniest dab of glue and touches the ox beetle's body. Then she picks up the broken-off leg with the tweezers.

She can hear Cody breathing slowly. He must be concentrating on the dead bug surgery as hard as she is. She touches the top of the leg to the drop of glue and positions it carefully. She holds it in place a few seconds before releasing her grip of the tweezers. "There. That looks pretty natural."

"Ahhhh!" Cody screams. "They're stuck! My fingers are stuck forever!" He holds them close to the little window in the magnifying hood, showing her a giant thumb and first finger glued in a permanent pinch.

"Cody, I warned you!" When she lifts the hood, he's crying. "Don't worry. Miss J will be home in half an hour. She'll think of something."

To stop his crying, Anna pours Cody a soda. He slurps the whole glass down before telling her he's not allowed to have soda. "It makes me hyper," he informs her.

It isn't long before he seems to be used to having two of his major digits glued together. Sugar-charged, he buzzes around the room. "Sea dagger!" he exclaims, looking at the seed floating in its water glass on the shelf over the sink. "They have those in the Keys."

"Mica sent it. Are you sure you can't pull your fingers apart?"

Cody tries again, but the skin just stretches. "How come you have a 2 on your hand?"

"It's for a club I'm in with Mica." *It should really be the Club of 3 if it's me, Mica, and Colleen,* she thinks. And, although she looked the word up, she can't figure out what Mica meant about being *pro*karyotic. If it's a joke, she's on the outside. She wonders if letting her into the Club of 2 means that Colleen gets to be a Sorta Sister too. Anna doesn't want to hurt Colleen's feelings, but she hopes not.

"Can I join the club?" Cody asks. "Mica's my friend too. Or is this like Ben's stupid clubs—big kids only?"

Anna knows how he feels; she's usually the one left out. She inks a 2 on the back of his glued hand.

Dear Mica,

This is an ox beetle <u>(Strategus antaeus)</u>. Cody found it. A leg broke off when Beauty knocked the box with the beetle in it out of his hand. While I glued the leg back on, Cody glued his fingers together. We had to wait around for Miss J to come home. She unstuck him with acetone.

I hope you don't mind but I let Cody join the Club of 2. He said you like him. Does that make it the Club of 4?

And now for the Mr. Webster report. Miss J and I went on another date with him. He took us out for Chinese at the Super Buffet. You never know what you'll find at the Super Buffet. Tonight there was a tray of poached chicken feet. That's right. Chicken feet. I counted them the first time we filled our plates. Thirteen. And I counted them when we went back for dessert. Still thirteen. Mr. Webster said that meant there were six regular chickens and one peg-legged pirate chicken. Then he picked up the extra leg with the tongs and said, "May I recommend the chicken foot?" Miss J liked the idea of cooking chicken feet because it meant they didn't get wasted. But I noticed that she didn't eat one.

Three on a date is one too many. I told Miss J that when she and I went to get seconds of fried rice. She said when I start dating she plans to go on <u>all</u> my dates.

I hoped my fortune cookie would give me good news. It didn't. On the "Learn Chinese" side of the little paper was the Chinese word for Europe, "Ou zhou." On the fortune side it said, "Change is the greatest teacher." Things have changed enough in my life.

Your Sorta Sister,
Anna

p.s. Thanks for letting me in the Club of 2. Does that mean Colleen is a Sorta Sister? She can be if you want, but it seems like it should be just you and me—we're the ones without real brothers and sisters. She probably has some.

p.p.s. Say hi to Colleen.

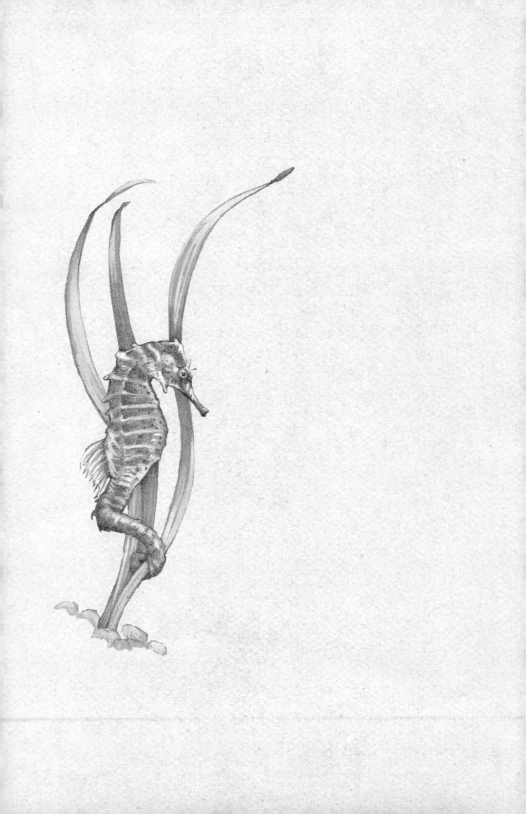

chapter 13

"IT'S SAT-UR-DAY—NO SCHOOL, Colleen's coming over—girls rule," Mica sings. There are too many syllables in the second part, and she got the "girls rule" off a T-shirt she saw in the hall at PKS, but nothing bothers her today. Her friend is coming over!

She's washed the breakfast dishes, straightened out the sleeping bag on her bed, and swept the deck. When she double-checks the deck, she spots the Captain's underpants on the wash line strung from bow to stern. Oh man. Not a good idea for Colleen to see his tightie-whities! Not bothering to pinch the tops of the clothespins, she jerks the underpants off the line—*snap, snap, snap.* They're stiff from drying in the sun.

As she scrambles below deck and crunches them into the drawer under his bunk, a new verse for her song pops into her head. "It's Sat-ur-day—no class. School's a big fat pain in the…butt." Mica smiles to herself.

Dr. Winn doesn't use the lab on weekends, so the Captain is at work. He hasn't met Colleen, and Mica doesn't mind if it stays that way. She loves the Captain, but she has to admit that he isn't very tactful.

He wouldn't chant "ooga-wagah, ooga-wagah" like the boys at school do when Colleen walks by. He'd be more likely to say

"Amazing thing, the human body. There isn't another species that shows such a wide range of body shapes."

In other words, *ooga-wagah, ooga-wagah.*

But the fact that her dad won't be here almost torpedoed the visit. Colleen's mother is strict. No adult supervision, no visit. "Aunt Emma will be there," Mica claimed as the steam from a tray of lunchroom meatloaf rose between them. She didn't bother to explain what kind of aunt Aunt Emma was. The word "aunt" reassured Mrs. Farrell.

Mica rifles through the dock box and fishes out masks and snorkels. She sets them on the picnic table beside the *Martina*. Colleen can use the black mask. The blue one leaks. To make the good mask look better, she polishes the glass with the tail of her T-shirt and a little spit.

She puts the mask on to check for streaks and ends up looking through it at the bubbling aquariums on the table. The first holds two seahorses she collected. Both are a dabby brown to match the strands of turtle grass they cling to. Their tiny, conical eyes swivel her way. Both seahorses are male. The Captain says she should release one, but even seahorses need company. "Colleen's coming over," she whispers.

Suddenly she remembers the letter from Anna that arrived yesterday, the one with the ox beetle in it. She pops the mask off her face and drops it on the picnic table. She jumps back into the *Martina*'s galley and sweeps the ox beetle into the tin it arrived in. She and the Captain thought it looked good sitting on top of the weather radio, but not knowing Colleen's opinion of bugs, Mica can't take a chance. "Sorry, Anna," she says, and stuffs the tin in her laundry bag.

At the other end of the state of Florida, Anna opens her eyes and stares at the ceiling above her bed. The good news: It's Saturday. The bad news: The phone's ringing, and when Miss J picks up Anna can tell by the gladness in her voice that Mr. Webster is calling with some great plan for their day. She tries to imagine herself down in the Keys aboard the boat with Mica, but it's getting harder because it isn't just Mica and Anna anymore. Mica mentioned that Colleen planned to come over, and Saturday is the day for coming over. Being with Mica *and* Colleen is too much like the rest of her life.

She tries to burrow back into sleep, but Beauty's toenails click across the floor. *Whump.* The dog jumps on the bed.

"The river's waiting!" Miss J yells from the hallway.

Anna opens one eye. "Waiting for who?"

Miss J stands in her bedroom door, one of *Lulu II*'s paddles in each hand. "Us. The girls. You, me, and Beauty."

Anna sits up, hugging her blanket-covered knees. "Are Mr. Webster and Trog meeting us?"

"Nope. If you ever get your lazy self out of that bed, it's Girls' Day on the Wakulla River. Says so right on the calendar."

Anna's bare feet hit the cool wood floor. "Okay. Give me two minutes."

"Hurry up! Daylight's wasting. We'll eat quick and load the canoe."

Anna hums as she pulls on a T-shirt and jeans. The day ahead unwinds, becoming the bright silvery ribbon of the Wakulla River.

They're lashing the canoe to the rack on Miss J's Volkswagen when the phone starts to ring inside the house. "Ignore it," says Miss J, tightening a bungee cord.

But the phone rings and rings. Anna imagines that she's the one at the other end of the line, listening and hoping someone will pick up. "I'll get it." She dashes inside with Beauty at her heels. She has just put her hand on the phone when the answering machine picks up and her own voice says, "You have reached the home of Miss Johnette and Anna. We're not here but we promise to call you back really soon." *Beep.*

A man clears his throat. "Okay. Guess you're on your way to the river. Trog and I hope you have a good time—although he says to ask how that's possible without us! Listen. You think maybe we could stop by later?" He sounds as if he's waiting for an answer. Anna could pick up, but she doesn't. "Heck, I don't mean to push," he goes on. "Trog and I just need a little clarification. Is 'girls' day' a twenty-four-hour event or is it over when the sun goes down? Either way, give us a call."

Mr. Webster would be so happy if she picked the phone up and told him, meet us at the landing. Instead Anna listens until she hears the click of him hanging up. "Girls' Day is for girls," she tells Beauty. "And he's always here. This is our Saturday. We're taking turns. That's fair, right?"

"Who was it?" asks Miss J, putting the cooler on the back seat.

"Mr. Webster. He said to have a good time."

Mica dashes up the marina office steps. "How's the food coming along?"

Aunt Emma lowers the newspaper she's reading with a rattle. "It's in the soda case."

Mica slides open the glass door and sticks her head inside. Chicken salad on puffy white rolls! They even have frilly toothpicks holding them together. She whirls around. "Thank you, thank you for not getting healthy bread with sprouted thingamabobs in it. Colleen *hates* healthy things."

"I also bought cherries. I hope they're not too healthy for Colleen."

"Cherries are a good-healthy fruit." Mica perches on her usual stool, knees bouncing, too nervous to sit for long. She glances at the chip rack. "And we'll have chips, of course."

Her eyes slide over to the cake rack. The packaged dessert cakes are loaded with sugar and fat, so Emma restricts them. "Can we have Little Debbies for dessert, please?" Mica wheedles. "It's a special occasion."

"It *is* a special occasion. Much too special for cake in a plastic bag." Aunt Emma peels back the foil on a plate of cupcakes that sits on the tackle counter. "What do you think?"

"You made these yourself?"

"I got up extra early."

"How early, two years? You even drew little flowers on them with squirt icing!" Mica sort of wishes Aunt Emma hadn't gotten so carried away and written "Colleen" on one and "Mica" on another. It looks babyish. But she jumps off the stool and wraps her arms around Aunt Emma's neck. "Perfecto, Aunt Emmo! I'd better check again." She trots out the door.

"Your friend isn't due for half an hour," Aunt Emma calls after her.

Mica sticks her head back inside. "Does ten thirty mean ten thirty, or is that just an estimate?" She's never had a friend come for a planned visit before.

"It's good manners to be within fifteen minutes either way."

That means there's no chance that Colleen will arrive for at least fifteen more minutes. To distract herself, Mica eats three cupcakes. After that she dedicates herself to waiting for her friend nonstop.

It's ten forty-five when the Plantation Fisheries truck pulls off US 1. At the wheel is the same old guy who's been making deliveries as long as Mica's been at the marina. But today, waving at her through the passenger window is Colleen.

Mica dashes over and grabs the edge of the open window. "Hi!"

"Sorry we're late," Colleen huffs. "He has to talk to everyone!" She nods toward the driver. "So, anyway. This is my dad."

Mica says hi again.

The man reaches out a calloused hand. "Hi yourself, young lady." They shake across Colleen's lap. Colleen's dad looks older than the Captain, sun-baked and wrinkly. His hair and eyelashes are as pale as Colleen's.

Uncle Bert comes over to the truck, wiping his hands on a rag. "How's it goin', Sunny?"

"Can't complain," says Colleen's father. He climbs out and opens the back doors of the truck.

Mica puts both hands on the edge of the open window. She bounces on her toes. "Come on, get out. And why are you wearing a dress?"

"Mom made me. Just don't laugh." Colleen opens the door and Mica sees a pair of patent leather shoes and the stiff layered skirt of the dress.

"It looks like you're going to church!" Mica's never been, but she's seen Aunt Emma leave on Sunday morning in her fancy dress and tight shiny shoes. Mica thinks of church as a place where people go to show off new clothes and be uncomfortable.

"Why did your mom make you dress up?"

Colleen blows out her breath. "She said I should look nice."

"Well, you do…look nice, I mean."

"Would you be caught dead in puff sleeves?" Colleen lets her feet dangle out the car door, the patent leather gleaming like motor oil. "I mean, they're for five-year-olds. But Mom makes all my dresses with them."

Mica is wondering how many dresses Colleen has when her friend adds, "Puff sleeves are stupid."

"Totally stupid," Mica quickly agrees.

Colleen crosses her arms in satisfaction. "Thank you."

Mica feels closer than ever to Colleen now that they've agreed puffed sleeves are stupid. "Your swimsuit is underneath, right?"

Colleen pulls her feet back inside the truck cab. "You didn't say we were swimming!"

"Of course we are. This is a marina!" Mica realizes that she's yelling at her new best friend. She pauses to smile, then lowers her voice. "I thought you'd know it was what we were going to do. Anyway, it's okay. I guess we'll think of something else."

"Sure." Colleen slides across the seat and jumps down, raising a cloud of dust that clings to the toes of her church shoes. Reaching back into the cab, she grabs a book off the seat. "We can read."

"Read? Reading's for when it's raining." Just then Mica has a totally inspired thought. "Say, Aunt Emma has a bunch of old swimsuits people left behind. I'll bet one would fit you."

Colleen backs toward the truck. "I don't know. Maybe I'd better just go with my dad."

"But why? The suits are ugly, but it's just us, the Club of 2!" She holds up her hand to show the faded but still legible 2.

They've been inking them on every morning, but Mica's keeps washing off in the canal.

For a moment Colleen stares at the 2. "I can't," she mumbles. "I can't because…" She takes a deep breath, unable to finish the sentence.

"Is it because…you know—" Aunt Emma gave her the "girl talk" just before school started.

"No!" Colleen blushes up to the roots of her hair. "It's just that…I can't swim, okay?"

Mica is dumbstruck. Colleen Farrell, born and raised in the Keys, can't swim. Then Mica realizes that if she acts all amazed Colleen will spend the rest of the day with her father, delivering bait to all the tackle stores and marinas between here and Key West. And she will get through the morning by sitting with Aunt Emma and eating cupcakes until she barfs. Mica casually rearranges the pea gravel with one bare big toe. "It's not hard," she says, glancing at Colleen through her bangs. "I could teach you."

Mica didn't think it was possible, but pale Colleen turns even paler. "Maybe," she whispers. "But not now. Later."

Anna kneels in the bow of the red canoe. Miss J kneels in the stern. The wind is in their faces as they paddle down the river. Beauty's in the middle—in what they call the "Queen of the Nile" position. Whoever sits there gets to ride without doing any of the work. Beauty must not know she's the queen. She thinks it's her job to bark at other canoes and at any bird that flies by the *Lulu II*.

"Cut that out, Beauty," Miss J scolds.

"She's just guarding our river from everybody else." Anna reaches back and scruffs the thick fur on Beauty's neck.

"But she scares off all the wildlife."

"She'll learn. She's new at being a biology dog." Miss J's old retriever, Gregor Mendel, seemed to understand everything. Miss J used to say that if only he could talk he'd offer scientific opinions of his own.

A kingfisher glides across the river and Beauty raises a howl. Miss J is hushing her again when the surface of the water beside the canoe bulges and a dark, glossy mound rises as if suddenly, here in the middle of the river, they're about to go aground.

Anna grips the gunwale with both hands. "Miss J?" she whispers.

"Mercy!" Miss J whispers back. "It's a manatee. I hope to heck Beauty doesn't see her."

As the manatee rolls on her side, a whiskery muzzle and one small eye break the surface. The eye is embedded in thick wrinkled skin, like a pebble pressed into hot tar. "She's looking at you!" Miss J says softly.

Anna leans toward the water. The eye blinks shut, then opens.

"Bet you look as strange to her as she does to you," Miss J adds.

"She's not strange," Anna breathes, "she's beautiful." Anna and the manatee are studying each other when Beauty jumps to her feet, tail stiff, and lets out an ear-splitting howl.

"Beauty!" Miss J clamps a hand on the dog's collar.

Only Anna sees the eye wink shut as the manatee submerges slowly. Miss J is scolding Beauty for being an irresponsible barker when Anna says, "Look! There's another one, under the big one."

The smaller, lighter shape floats below the adult. "That's her calf," says Miss J. "Too bad Jonah's not here. He would've loved to see that. Manatees are a big favorite of his."

Anna feels guilty. He would be here if she had picked up the phone. She grabs the paddle and digs it into the water. It's *her* day. She deserves a day.

But suddenly keeping the day to herself feels like eating a whole box of candy without sharing. *But it's just one day,* she thinks. *One.*

"I'm done." Mica stuffs the last bite of cupcake in her mouth.

"Me too." Colleen unties the ribbon around the waist of her dress. "I am totally satiated."

Mica spread the lunch out on the counter as soon as they got inside because she didn't know what else to do. They had to get to "later" somehow. But now there's no more eating they can do and Colleen has only been at Bert's Marina for twenty-three minutes.

"Want to swim?" Mica asks.

"Can't." Colleen smiles with crumbs on her lips. "We just ate."

"That stuff about cramps isn't even true," Mica starts, but she can see that Colleen believes in cramps—or at least pretends she does so she doesn't have to swim. "Okay, we'll wait. But…what do you want to do now?"

After a long pause, Aunt Emma starts asking questions. That's how Mica finds out that Colleen has an older brother named George who works for the fish house too. When she says she wishes she had a brother, Colleen wrinkles her nose. "He always smells like mullet."

That's also how Mica learns that Colleen wants to be an English professor. To Mica teaching English makes as much sense as teaching breathing lessons. "What's there to teach about English?"

Colleen holds her nose up in the air. "Literature."

"You have mayonnaise on your chin," Mica points out.

Colleen swipes at it with the back of her hand. "My aunt Connie teaches literature at Johns Hopkins University in Baltimore. I spend every summer with her."

Mica feels her best plan ever slip away like a fish getting off the hook. "*Every* summer?" She'd imagined them hanging out together once school was over. When Colleen had rolled up in the bait truck that morning, the plan had seemed even more perfect. Colleen's dad could swing into the marina at the start of his route and drop Colleen off. "Do you have to go *this* summer?" she asks.

Colleen rolls her eyes. "You'd have to chain me to a rock to get me to stay here."

Mica kicks at a rung of her stool. "What's so great about Baltimore?"

"Everything. The zoo…the aquarium—"

"Big deal," Mica interrupts. "You *live* in an aquarium."

"In Baltimore we have the *National* Aquarium. But the best thing is the Enoch Pratt Free Library."

"We have a library!"

"Dinky," says Colleen with a sniff. "Besides, I've read everything in it already."

It's time to change the subject. Mica thinks about suggesting that they go aboard the *Martina*, but the tide is full. Colleen might have a hard time climbing up onto the boat. She considers suggesting a visit to the shrimp tank instead, but after the National Aquarium, why would Colleen want to look at a few pink shrimp?

Out of ideas, Mica folds her hands on the counter and listens to Colleen drone on to Aunt Emma about the wonders of the fantasy section at the Free Library.

Dear Anna,

The Captain begged me to quit talking about Colleen's visit. He said, "Write all of this down and send it to Anna," meaning "I'm tired of hearing about it." So get comfortable. This could take a while.

The Club of 2 had its first official meeting at Bert's Marina—wish you had been here because it was almost a disaster. Colleen knows more about places in books than she does about the Keys. She can't even swim! And she thinks sharks are lurking everywhere.

For the longest time all we did was sit around the marina office and talk and eat and talk some more and eat some more. Aunt Emma and I taught her to play rummy. Colleen whipped our butts—and won half the pennies in our jars.

Aunt Emma and I finally convinced her to put on a swimsuit some visitor left in the marina shower. The elastic was dead. It made her look like an old elephant. Since Colleen can't swim, Aunt Emma gave her a pair of brand-new water wings from the marina store. I threw the wrapping out before

Colleen could see the part of the label that said "Safe for children up to forty pounds." Colleen reads everything.

You know how slow tectonic plates move? That's how long it took us to get in the water. First Colleen stopped to look at the specimens in the aquariums. She said the seahorses were like miniature dragons. (Dragons don't exist, but Colleen knows everything about them.) Then we sat on the dock with our feet in the water until our backs got so hot you could fry eggs on them.

For the next eon we stood in the shallow water by the dock. First Colleen didn't like the way the bottom oozed between her toes. Then she wouldn't move because she was afraid a crab was going to pinch her. I was sure her father would get back from driving bait down to Key West before we got our suits wet.

We were up to our knees when Aunt Emma yelled over to us to get out so she could put more sunscreen on Colleen. I knew if we got out we'd never get back in. So we kept inching. We were only up to our waists when the Captain came roaring home on his scooter. He was in a pretty good mood, so he swam with us and even made up a stupid game called Motorboat. He let Colleen put her arms around his neck and towed her out to the middle of the canal. He helped her float on her back a while, and then we dragged her in.

He got her to take off the water wings and do a few splashy strokes, but then her dad came to get her. I begged him to let her stay longer. We were having a great time! But her mom was fixing supper. (Eating together is important at her house.) Maybe next time she can spend the night.

Colleen found this shell (She thought it was about to bite her foot!) while we were standing in the ooze. It's a tulip shell <u>(Fasciolaria tulipa)</u>. It's pretty, but if you're a whelk or a conch, look out! Tulips are fierce predators. The best thing about this shell is that it's clean, which means that the tulip died a while ago (no stink). The better thing is that it doesn't have a hermit crab in it—a hermit <u>would</u> have pinched her foot. Add it to your collection!

Your CO^2 friend,
Mica

chapter 14

MICA HASN'T SEEN—OR EVEN TALKED TO—Colleen since her visit on Saturday. The Captain doesn't believe in cell phones. The rare times he has to communicate with the outside world, he uses the pay phone sitting in the corner of the marina's parking lot. Even though the sun beats down on the glass and turns the metal box into an oven, Mica traded fifty pennies from her jar for two quarters and tried to call her friend yesterday. The teenager who answered (probably George) said, "Colleen's at Sunday school. Is this Mica?" She said uh-huh and hung up fast, but she was thrilled. Colleen's brother knew her name.

Mica picks up the new backpack Aunt Emma bought her. "Come on, come on!" she urges the Captain.

He pours himself a second cup of coffee. "Why the rush?"

"School, remember? S-C-H-O-O-L! I'm going to be late."

"I must say, this is quite a change of heart!" He turns his wrist and takes a leisurely look at his watch. "Plenty of time."

"Don't you want to get to the lab?" she coaxes. The Captain is always happiest when he's studying nature in a controlled environment. But he takes another slow sip. "Okay, I'll be waiting for you up top. But hurry." Mica stomps up the ladder to the deck, the backpack slapping her shoulders.

Topside, the deck is wet with dew so she doesn't sit. She already knows what kids say when you show up at school with a wet butt. The usual dragonflies perch on the ropes that droop from stanchion to stanchion, looking as lazy as the Captain. She twangs a rope, sending the dragonflies wheeling out over Snake Creek.

She's about to put on her helmet when she remembers the letter to Anna in the top of her pack. Maybe Aunt Emma will mail it. She slides the hatch back and pokes her head through. "Drink fast!" she calls down to the Captain. Then she sprints to the office and shoves the letter at Aunt Emma. "Mail this, please?"

Aunt Emma frowns at the lump in the middle of the envelope. "I hope this isn't fragile."

"It's a tulip shell. They're sturdy. It's wrapped in gobs of toilet paper. Plus, I wrote the mail guys a note that'll take care of it. Gotta go. Bye."

As she trots back from the marina office, Mica can see that the moped is still leaning against a piling. She runs to the *Martina's* galley window and presses her forehead against the screen until it bulges. "Captain! Hurry! Up!" She retrieves her helmet from the picnic table and shakes out a spider. By the time the Captain appears on deck, she's standing by the scooter, her helmet on her head, a new 2 Magic-Markered on her hand.

Getting on and off the boat is hard for her father, but sometimes it seems as if he exaggerates the limp as an excuse to go slower. She can't say anything. Telling him to hurry only makes his limp worse.

But once they're on the scooter, they fly. Arms around his waist, she rests her cheek on his back. They curve into the school's drop-off lane. The bike is slowing to a wobble when Mica hops off. "Bye." She stuffs the helmet in the pack and dashes for Mrs. Bohannon's homeroom, bursting to ask Colleen to come over to swim again.

She stops just inside the classroom door. A knot of kids surrounds Colleen's desk. No one ever pays attention to Colleen, except to knock her stuff on the floor. Now everyone is paying attention.

"Looks like she's gonna pop," says Mark.

"Even worse than usual," Joel agrees.

Mica elbows between them and sees Colleen's puffy red face gleaming with some kind of slimy green lotion.

"She's shiny like a balloon with too much air in it," says Stephanie.

Mica turns on them. "Get away from her. Get away!" They're all talking about Colleen like she's a thing, not a person. "What's wrong with you morons? Haven't you ever seen a sunburn before?"

Colleen won't look up. Mica drops to her knees in front of her friend's assigned seat. "I'm sorry, Colleen. I didn't know you'd fry. I never burn."

Tears quiver on Colleen's cheeks. "You're tan. I'm not! Aunt Emma *told* you I needed more sunscreen." Colleen lowers her head onto her folded arms, wincing when her burnt forehead touches her sleeve. Face hidden, she sits perfectly still.

Mica doesn't know what to do about Colleen, but she does know what to do about the jerks who are glued to the scene as if she and Colleen were a soap opera. She jumps to her feet and pushes the nearest kid, who happens to be Joel. He's a foot and a half taller than she is and heavy, so she doesn't expect him to fall down. But he does.

"Miss Delano!" When did Mrs. Bohannon walk into the classroom? The teacher strides over, clamps a hand on Mica's shoulder, and turns her toward the door. "Double-time, young lady! March!"

Mica doesn't have to ask where she's double-timing to. She can practically follow her own pheromone trail.

After an interesting lecture from the principal on self-restraint, Mica walks to first period with a hall pass in her hand and a request for a parent conference in the front flap of her pack. She doesn't care. As she pushes the classroom door open, the students' glances swarm her like no-see-ums. The only one who doesn't look her way is Colleen.

Lunchtime comes and they still haven't spoken or traded a single look. Mica walks to the cafeteria slowly. By the time she sets her plastic tray on the stainless steel ledge, Colleen is back in her old spot, alone at the end of a table.

Without Colleen for a friend, she isn't even hungry for her favorite school lunch—ham with pineapple slices—and she doesn't want to talk to Colleen's mom, who is probably mad at her too.

She keeps her head down as she pushes the tray along and formulates a plan. To avoid suspicion she'll go through the lunch motions. She'll grab a plate of hot lunch, pay for it, and then walk straight past Colleen's table to the maze of garbage cans. She'll dump the food and leave the empty tray on top of the others waiting to be washed. And then she'll break out of PKS.

But she'll do it right this time. She won't run. And she won't talk back to Day-Glo Strap. She'd tried that her third day at school. "What are you keeping us safe from?" she'd asked when he told her the strap meant Safety Patrol. "Kids with sharp pencils?" Big deal. He'd written her up. But a failed escape attempt might have real consequences.

Today she'll walk silently to the door. But if Day-Glo Strap commands her to halt, she'll run at the push bar and hit it and she won't quit running until she's off school property. The Day-Glo kid won't come after her. Not leaving school property without permission is encoded in his DNA. Let him write her up and report her to the principal. By then she'll be walking home, whistling.

But that's later. Now she's pushing a tray and not looking up. Still, she knows this is the moment of ultimate danger because she smells ham patties and pineapple and feels damp steam on her face.

She hunches her shoulders and tries to get past Mrs. Farrell without being noticed.

"Mica?" Because the voice sounds friendly, she looks up. Colleen's mother is holding out a plate with extra ham and extra pineapple on it. And Mica knows instantly that Mrs. Farrell isn't mad at her. Mrs. Farrell makes it clear she likes you by what she puts on your plate. "Sure that's enough?" she asks.

"Yes, ma'am." Mica's resolve to dump the tray and escape is weakening—maybe she'll just eat first. She pays the cashier and her feet take her to her regular spot—the spot where she sat alone for the first few days of school. The spot she shared with Colleen after that. She sets the tray down, but doesn't sit. Instead she looks at Colleen.

Colleen seems to be watching her. It's hard to see her eyes because her sunburned face is so puffy. No wonder she's mad. She *does* look like a balloon that's about to pop. But can she stay mad forever? Mica holds up her hand, showing Colleen the Magic Marker 2.

Colleen doesn't smile, doesn't budge. Still, Mica holds her

hand in the air. Slowly, slowly, Colleen raises her own hand. Even from three tables away, Mica can see the bold black 2.

With empty seats on either side of her, Colleen is like an island completely separated from the mainland of the rest of the school. If Mica sits down at her old table, she'll be an island too. Instead, Mica picks up her tray again and walks over to Colleen. Being an island won't be so bad as long as they are separate together.

"Is this seat taken?"

"Yeah, by the invisible man." Colleen gives her a halfway smile. "You can sit in his lap."

"Are you still mad?" Mica asks as she sets down her tray.

Colleen pushes a piece of pineapple around her plate with her plastic fork. "I was. Now I'm over it."

"I'm sorry you got burned. Does it hurt?"

"It feels like I have ants crawling all over me."

"That doesn't sound *so* bad."

But Colleen isn't going to let her off easy. "Fire ants."

"Oh. Sorry." Mica suddenly realizes how hungry she is. She stabs a chunk of ham with her fork. "You want to come over again on Saturday?"

"No. You come to my house. And *don't* bring your swimsuit."

chapter 15

"OH, HAPPY DAY!" JOHNETTE EXCLAIMS, pulling the letter from the Keys out of their mailbox. She knows Anna will light up when she sees it.

Even though the neighborhood is crawling with kids, local friends are kind of scarce. Anna never brings anyone home except Cody Floyd. Since Ben is spending all his time with a new girlfriend, Cody seems abandoned. Cody's a great kid, but even Johnette knows he's not the friend a seventh-grade girl would choose. Whether it's a dog or a lonely boy, big-hearted Anna tends to take in strays.

Too bad Mica Delano lives so far away, Johnette thinks, walking back to the house. *She seems like the kind of friend Anna would pick for herself.*

She finds Anna at the kitchen table, engrossed in writing in her explorer's notebook. The notebook went with her when her aunt and uncle put her into foster care. She writes in the notebook about all the places she's lived; she draws maps. Johnette hasn't seen her writing in it lately.

"Can you think of anything else?" Anna asks.

Johnette looks over Anna's shoulder and discovers that she's compiling a list of things they'll do if Mica visits this summer—which makes the timing of the letter perfect.

"Guess what I found in the mailbox!" She slaps Mica's letter down, smack in the middle of the list.

Anna sweeps it up and rips open the flap. When she lifts out the wad of toilet paper, something dusty and broken spills onto her notebook. "You think it used to be a shell?" Anna asks.

"Looks like it. Maybe we can glue it. We've got all the pieces."

Anna tips the envelope. The remaining sandy fragments scatter on the table.

"Guess not," Johnette says. "What kind of shell was it? We can at least look at a picture."

As Anna skims the letter, her shoulders slump. "Here it is at the very bottom. She says it's a tulip shell. *Fasciolaria tulipa*."

"*Fasciolaria tulipa*, coming right up!" Johnette goes to the living room where she ransacks the shelf of field guides. "Dang! Have you seen my *Seashells of North America*?"

"You lent it to Mr. Webster, remember? He didn't bring it back."

"Guess we'll have to charge him a late fee." Johnette sticks her head back in the kitchen. "And you can call him Jonah, you know."

"Or Big Guy or Mr. Science or Bio Man," Anna adds.

"So pick one!" says Johnette.

Anna closes the explorer's notebook and pushes it away. "To me he seems like a Mr. Webster."

"You could try dropping the mister." Johnette ducks into the living room again. "Does that sound okay?" All that comes back from the kitchen is silence, and Johnette wonders if Anna is avoiding the question or reading her letter. There's so much Johnette doesn't get about being a mom.

Solving the problem of the shell should be easier—but not having the right field guide slows her down. "Wait!" she declares.

"There's more than one way to skin a cat!" Then, thinking she might get a rise out of Anna, she adds, "Who'd want to skin a cat anyway?" She waits for a goofy comeback, but the kitchen remains silent.

She strides over to the rolltop desk she inherited from her father and hits the "on" button on her computer. While she waits for it to boot up, Johnette tries to remember if she had silences at Anna's age. If she did, it was only because she wasn't around people that much. She was usually busy foraging for specimens in the swamp near her home or holed up in her room adding the specimens to her "Complete Insects of Florida" collection. Her mother probably thought she was quiet too—Johnette knows for sure her mom didn't think it was healthy for a girl to spend all her free time catching bugs, killing them with nail polish remover fumes, and sticking pins through their dead bodies.

She is typing *Fasciolaria tulipa* into Google when she has another thought. Maybe something in the letter is the problem. "I could use a little entertainment while I hunt for a picture of this used-to-be shell," she calls out. "What's Mica got to say?"

As Anna reads the letter in a dull monotone, Johnette aches for her foster daughter. Of course Mica's glad to have a new friend, but does she have to rub it in? Luckily Johnette finds a picture of the shell just as Mica is signing off. "Got it!" she yells, hitting "print." This will distract Anna.

"*Fasciolaria tulipa!*" she announces as she strides back into the kitchen. "I found that bad boy on Google images." She hands Anna the print of a pretty brown and white shell.

Anna's glance grazes the printout, but settles on the pile of shell chips and dust. "It wouldn't have broken if she'd wrapped it better." She pushes the chair back and goes to the sink. Boosting herself on the edge of the counter, she reaches up and turns the sea dagger in the glass on a high shelf above the sink. The shoot, which has grown two leaves, has been bending hard toward the window. Now it points into the kitchen.

"Good idea," Johnette says. "Give it some exercise."

"It probably can't grow here anyway."

This isn't a bit like Anna. Anna—a born optimist—would be more likely to believe that by the middle of next week they'll have a full-sized mangrove shading the kitchen sink than to say it isn't going to make it. "Took it a while to get started," Johnette says, "but it seems to be doing fine." She glances down at Mica's letter. "Bet you would've liked to be there with Mica and Colleen."

Anna's shoulders lift and drop. "Not really. Three's a crowd." She turns and walks slowly toward the door. "I'm going to my room now. To make my bed."

Johnette flashes a smile at Anna's back. "Hey! You're making me look bad!" (She hasn't made her own bed yet.) She watches Anna walk out of the kitchen and across the living room. The girl looks like a plant in need of a good watering.

Beauty, who follows at her heels, droops too. This is not a good sign. Johnette might fool herself into thinking Anna's okay, but dogs know unhappy when they see it. Dogs don't let their brains get in the way.

Anna makes her bed carefully and curls up on top of the spread. She feels the mattress give as Beauty slinks up. The dog crams herself as close as she can get to Anna.

A tongue licks Anna's neck. "You're a messy kisser, girl!" But she throws an arm across Beauty's neck. "What did you think of that letter?" she whispers. "I thought there were *way* too many Colleens."

Colleen spent the day at Bert's Marina.

Colleen ate lunch with Aunt Emma and Mica on the tackle counter.

Colleen swam in the boat basin.

Colleen. Colleen. Colleen.

Anna wants to be happy that Mica found a friend who's right there. She could use one of those herself. But she'd feel okay about it—or *more* okay—if it weren't for the crushed shell. The shell was thrown in like an afterthought. Mica didn't even put it in a box.

Colleen and Mica: The Club of 2.

The 2 says it all.

Anna is tired of being the extra one, the one who always gets dumped.

After her parents died she was passed around her family, then she ended up with Social Services. Her first foster mom, Miss Dupree, fell in love. Anna never understood that expression until she saw it happen to Miss Dupree. She acted like Cupid shot her through the heart. *Wham!* Down she went. In no time at all Miss Dupree was engaged and handing her off to Miss Johnette.

Now Anna's afraid it will happen again because of Mr. Webster. Miss J says no. She promises that she and Anna will be a family forever. Anna knows that Miss J means what she says, but like paper covers rock, falling in love might beat a promise.

Anna's staring at the ceiling when she hears a timid knock. Beauty lets out a single *woof.* Maybe Miss J wants to talk. But the knock didn't sound like Miss J, who does everything loud. At the second knock, Beauty jumps off the bed and runs barking to the window. That's when Anna realizes that someone outside is looking at her lying splat on her bed! She sits up fast. Cody's face is pressed against the glass, his nose flat. Anna stomps over and pushes the window up a few inches. "What are you doing?"

"Nothing. Want to come outside?"

"You should knock on the front door, not go around peeping in windows."

"Why not? You have your clothes on."

"But what if I didn't?"

"Gross!" He makes a gagging sound.

"Not as gross as if *you* didn't have *yours* on!"

"Oh yeah. Like I'd walk over here without my clothes on."

The screen is missing. He pushes the window up a little higher and sticks his head inside. "Mind if I come in?"

"Cody!"

Suddenly he whispers, "Shhh. I hear something." He pulls his head back outside, looking important.

She sticks her own head out the window and watches him tiptoe to the corner of the house and peer around. Still on tiptoe, he comes back. "A truck just pulled into your driveway. It's Mr. Webster and Trog." He hustles back to the corner and watches for a long minute, everything but his red high-tops twisted around the corner of the house. He pulls back to report. "Now Miss J is with him. The three of them are sitting on the tailgate."

"Who's in the middle?"

"Miss J."

Anna can usually count on Trog to worm between them, but the dog must be getting soft. "What are they doing?"

Cody looks down at his sneakers. "I dunno. Mostly talking."

Anna pushes the window up as far as it will go. "What do you mean, mostly?" She puts a foot on the windowsill, grabs the frame with both hands, and steps up. The opening isn't very big, but she's skinny. She limbos under the bottom edge and drops into the bed of ferns. She joins Cody at the corner of the house and peeks around. Miss J and Mr. Webster are gazing at each other.

Cody makes a kissing sound on the back of his hand.

Anna grabs his T-shirt and jerks him back. "Let's go climb our tree." She's being very generous and a little disloyal to Miss J by calling it "our tree," but Miss J is acting all "Club of 2" with Mr. Webster.

"Yeah," says Cody, sensing the change. "Let's climb *our* tree."

Cody rests the back of his head against the trunk and stares at the scolding squirrel in the crown of the tree. "He's mad all right. He says it's *his* tree." But Anna's watching the pickup in the driveway. Still seated on the tailgate, Miss J is swinging her legs. Mr. Webster laughs and picks up one of her hands.

Miss J says something, then glances at the house. She tries to wiggle her hand free, but Anna notices she isn't trying very hard. When he traps her hand between both of his she stops fighting and smiles up at him. According to Miss J, looking up at a guy is a nice change. All her life she's been called a "big girl." Jonah Webster is the first man she's ever dated who's taller than she is. But Anna can tell that her foster mom likes lots of things about him, not just his height, and that scares her.

Unaware that they're being watched, Miss J and Mr. Webster sit quietly, both looking at their joined hands as if they've just discovered them. Miss J shifts a little. The triangle of light between them disappears as she leans against him.

"Look out," Cody says softly. "They're gonna kiss."

158

"No, they're not!

"You watch."

"Hey!" Anna yells. "Up here!" She waves wildly.

Miss J drops Mr. Webster's hand and waves back. When Mr. Webster slumps, Miss J gives him a shove and jumps off the tailgate. In a second they're racing for the backyard.

"Beat ya!" says Miss J as she tags the tree.

Mr. Webster bends forward and stands with his hands on his thighs. "No fair," he pants. "I demand a rematch!"

"Okay, race you to the top of the tree!" Miss J scrambles up the ladder.

"I give up," he says, laughing. "You win."

Miss J turns and parks her butt on the first branch. "Don't you dare wimp out on me, Jonah Webster. Get up here!"

"You just discovered my big secret. I'm a tree-climbing wimp. My motto is, you can't fall out of a tree unless you climb one."

"But you have to!" Cody shouts at him. "It's easy for boys. Boys can climb."

"You hear that?" Miss J teases. "Boys can climb."

"Only for you, Johnette. I'd only do this for you." He puts a foot on the bottom rung. "You know, I should be influencing you, not the other way around. It's dangerous for kids to climb trees."

"Our ancestors lived in trees," Anna calls to him.

"Yeah, but we climbed down!" he yells back. "We evolved!"

chapter 16

Monday, March 24

EMMA CAN'T REMEMBER EVER SEEING Mica this nervous or excited, not even when she was getting ready for Colleen's visit.

"How do I look?" Mica stands, arms spread, in the middle of the marina office.

"You look fine, honey." Honestly, Emma could shoot Dr. Robin Michael Delano, world-famous marine biologist. He finally agreed to buy his daughter new clothes, then gave her no guidance at all. Emma understands he's a man. What guidance could he have given? But she offered to go along, and he turned her down. According to Mica, he stood outside the dressing room and urged her to hurry. Now Emma realizes that Mica has been wearing too-small clothes for so long that she went overboard the other way. So even though Mica's wearing the right kind of shirt (a pink T-shirt with a sparkly rose on the front) and the right kind of shorts (denim with lots of pockets), she still looks wrong.

Mica checks the back view of her reflection in the glass doors of the cooler. "Do I look like a fly swallowed by a Venus flytrap?"

"No." Aunt Emma can say that honestly because she's never seen a Venus flytrap—but Mica *does* look like she's being swallowed by something. "You'll grow into them before you know it."

"Maybe by the end of spring break." Mica grins. "I have this whole week off!" She's only been in school for a month and a half, but she's developed a healthy appreciation for days off.

Good, thinks Emma. *Before going to school the child never even realized what a vacation was. Since every day was a day off, Mica took them for granted.* She holds up an envelope, wondering if Mica is beginning to take her pen pal for granted too. "Don't forget about Anna's letter. Before you go to Colleen's you should open it."

"Later." Mica spins the chip rack.

A month ago Mica would've begged Emma to take her to the post office. She would've danced across the post office floor when she discovered that the box contained a letter from Tallahassee. Today she was too busy getting ready for her visit to Colleen's to think about Anna. "Aren't you the least bit curious? The letter's thick in the middle."

"I can't concentrate on a letter right now. I'm too nervous!"

"You aren't going to Colleen's for forty-five more minutes."

Mica spins the chip rack again, this time so hard the little bags stand straight out.

"I could read it to you."

Mica wanders over to the counter. "Okay."

Aunt Emma slices the envelope open with a fillet knife. A handful of dry brown leaves falls out.

Mica looks bored. "Just leaves?"

"Let's see what Anna says about them. Remember the fern she sent you? Things aren't always what they seem." Emma lowers her glasses and begins to read.

Dear Mica,

Do you understand adults? I hope so, because I need you
to explain them to me. Why do adults say things they don't
mean? Miss J is so honest most of the time, but she acts
really strange when I ask her about Mr. Webster. I think she
LIKES him but when I ask she says he's just a friend.

Why doesn't she say she likes him and get it over with?
Unless she doesn't.

But she must. He comes over all the time. She even puts on
perfume for him.

Today Cody and I were up in the Old Senator. Miss J and
Mr. Webster were sitting on the back of his truck, "talking."
When they saw us, Miss J decided to climb the tree too.
That's nothing new. When it's just the two of us, she climbs
the Old Senator all the time. But she dared Mr. Webster to
climb up with her.

Mr. Webster is built like a bear, but bears can do
something he can't—climb trees. He made it to the top of the
ladder and that's where he stayed, with his feet on the

ladder and his butt on the lowest branch—even Cody went higher. It was embarrassing!

Do you think it's possible for an excellent tree climber like Miss J to LIKE a man who can't make it past the first branch? I'm serious.

The leaves in this letter are oak leaves from the highest branch I've ever reached. I don't know what you can do with them. Maybe throw them in the ocean and confuse the fish.

Your SS,

Anna

p.s. That shell you sent got pulverized. Can you wrap the next one better?

Boring letter, Mica thinks. *Boring leaves.* She scoops them up and trots them out to the deck. Following Anna's suggestion, she tosses them into the basin. Minnows hit the leaves as if they were food, pushing them across the surface of the water. She'd usually find fooling the fish highly entertaining. Today it's only good for killing another two minutes.

"Mica?" Aunt Emma has followed her onto the deck, the boring letter in her hand. "It sounds as if Anna needs cheering up. You have a few minutes before we go. Why don't you write her?"

"I'll write her later." Sometimes Aunt Emma is as pushy as school. "Can you drive me now?"

Aunt Emma rests her plump arms on the railing and gazes at the *Martina.* "Shouldn't you tell the Captain you're leaving?"

"He knows." Her father is asleep, and probably will be for a few more hours. Mica left a note, which is getting to be the way they communicate. She wonders if he's okay—the thought nibbles at her, like the minnows nibbling at Anna's leaves, but she can't worry about him now, not when she's going to spend the day at Colleen's. "I'm ready. So, can we go?"

Aunt Emma checks her watch. "It's still a little early—"

"Early's good!" Mica dashes through the office and out the door on the other side, yelling, "Uncle Bert! Listen for the phone and keep an eye on the store. We're going to Colleen's!"

She finds him under the awning on the side of the marina pulling spark plugs. "I'll listen from out here." He gives her a wink. "Have yourself a good time, okay? Don't drink or cuss."

"Maybe I will, and maybe I won't." She winks back.

But as she climbs into the truck, she wonders what she *will* do at Colleen's. She already knows they won't be swimming. Since Mica swims all the time, *not* swimming is kind of exciting.

Aunt Emma fiddles with the key ring—she has lots of keys to who-knows-what, so it always takes her a while, but today it aggravates Mica. "It's the same one as always!" Mica blurts out, then bites her lip. "Sorry." She waits for Emma to start the van, then politely adds, "Turn south, okay?" But as soon as they're on the road she's urging Aunt Emma to go faster. "You're driving at snail speed!"

Accelerating to snail speed times two, Aunt Emma drives across the drawbridge at Snake Creek, then across the bridge at Whale Harbor.

"She lives in Parkerville. It's past the Green Turtle."

"I know where Parkerville is." Aunt Emma smiles and adds, "Parkerville is a real old neighborhood. The homes there were built by Conchs back before the Keys got expensive and crowded. The houses are tiny."

"I like small houses," Mica says loyally. Colleen's mom works in the school cafeteria; her dad drives a bait truck. How rich could they be? It doesn't bother Mica. She and the Captain aren't exactly rich either.

Aunt Emma pulls the truck between a pair of coral boulders and up a short drive. Mica blinks in surprise. The house is small, but as pretty as a dollhouse, everything exact and miniature. The walls are the color of the water on the reef: a beautiful turquoisey blue. A bougainvillea vine climbs the walls and covers the roof. The hot pink flowers peek in the windows. A neat garden is edged with conch shells, each with its pink, flared lip standing up like the fin of a sailfish.

The moment Mica opens the truck door, Colleen trots out of the house, followed more slowly by her mom. "See, we're not too early!" she tells Aunt Emma.

While Mrs. Farrell trudges around to Aunt Emma's window

to invite her in for a glass of sweet tea, Colleen swoops Mica out of the van. "Come *on!*" she commands, as if they've wasted too much time already. She jogs ahead and holds the screen door.

Mica steps inside, turns in place once, and falls in love with her friend's life. Her own home, the *Martina*, is kept shipshape, the Captain's term for empty, empty, empty. But there are *things* in Colleen's house. Two side chairs and a plump sofa are covered in flowered fabric. Their flowered seats are crammed with patch-work pillows, and the pillows are embroidered with sayings: "Home Is Where the Heart Is" and "Home Sweet Home" and "There's No Place Like Home."

Against the window is an ancient black sewing machine with a partially pieced quilt hanging over the chair in front of it.

Mica is looking at the quilt when Colleen's mother comes into the house, fanning her face with her hand. "What a shame your aunt had to get back to the marina."

"She doesn't trust Uncle Bert to run the cash register." Mica smooths a finger over a satiny patch. "This is so pretty."

"Why, thank you! That's Colleen's wedding quilt."

"Mo-om!" Colleen complains. "I already told you, I'm never getting married. Come on, Mica. Let's go to my room."

But Mica, suddenly surrounded by a soft flowery smell, stays put. Her friend's mother is beside her, holding up the quilt so they can get a better look. "How long have you been working on it?" Mica asks, leaning toward her.

Colleen collapses into one of the stuffed chairs. "Only since Varda created the stars over Middle-earth!"

"Oh, hush, Colleen. A quilt takes time." Mrs. Farrell doesn't bother to look up from the quilt—Mica guesses they've had this discussion before. "Most of the scraps come from the clothes I've made for Colleen over the years."

Mica glances up at Mrs. Farrell's broad, sweet face. "You saved them?"

"Of course."

"Mom is obsessive," Colleen says.

Mica is stunned—all those years of saving! And if Mrs. Farrell saved scraps from all Colleen's clothes, she probably has Colleen's baby teeth too. Maybe even hair from her first haircut.

"Let me show you the rest of it." Mrs. Farrell unfolds the quilt top and shakes it out. For a second, before it drifts to the floor, Mica can see the threads hanging on the underside.

"Of course I won't quilt it until Colleen gets engaged."

"Never happen!" Colleen crosses her arms.

"Of course it will, sweetie."

"Never happened to Aunt Connie." Colleen slumps down in the chair and closes her eyes.

Mica kneels on the edge of the quilt top and runs a hand over the patches. "It's like your whole life's been saved, Colleen!"

Her friend drums her fingers on the arm of the chair.

Mica points out a patch with ducks printed on it. "Where did that piece come from?"

Mrs. Farrell smiles. "That's from a sundress I made Colleen when she was two."

Colleen's arm falls off the edge of the chair and hangs limp.

"What about this one?" Mica asks, rubbing a scrap of velvet.

"What was it, Colleen?" Mrs. Farrell raises her eyebrows. "Christmas?"

Colleen barely opens an eye. "Yes, Christmas. Very hot."

"And this one?" Mica asks.

"Oh, that's from Colleen's secret other life," Mrs. Farrell teases. "Colleen spends summers with my twin sister, Connie."

"The one in Baltimore," says Mica, remembering.

"The one who never got married," Colleen adds. "That patch is from a dress Aunt Connie bought me to go to the symphony. Aunt Connie doesn't sew."

"She most certainly does!" Mrs. Farrell gathers the quilt in her arms.

"Not anymore. She has better things to do. Want to go to my room?" Colleen asks abruptly.

"Go on." Mrs. Farrell hugs the quilt. "This is a girl visit. I'll fix some snacks."

Mica is helping Colleen's mother arrange the quilt on the back of the chair when she hears a volley of whistling, and a teenage boy comes out of a bedroom wearing nothing but a pair of cutoffs. The boy's hair is auburn, like Mrs. Farrell's—Colleen must have inherited her blond hair from her Dad. He's heavy like Colleen and her mom, but his fish-house muscles bunch when he puts his hands on his hips.

"Is this George?" Mica asks.

He spreads his arms. "Yes, this is George. The one and only."

Colleen tries to hustle Mica past him into her room.

"Come on, Leeny, aren't you going to introduce me to your friend before you drag her off to the cave?"

"I've told you a million times, don't call me Leeny!"

"Sorry, Leeny." He reaches out a hand. "Nice to meet you. Bet you're Mica."

"Put a shirt on," Colleen snaps. "You look disgusting!"

Living in marinas for as long as she can remember, Mica is used to guys with bare chests. When he gives her hand a friendly squeeze, Mica decides George is the nicest brother ever.

"Hey, Mica, just yell if you need me to rescue you from Leeny of the black lagoon," he calls as Colleen propels her toward a dark bedroom. Although the door is open, Mica has to cut through a curtain of beads that touches her face like cool rain. When they're both in the room, Colleen reaches between the swaying strands and slams the door. "He is *such* a pain."

Mica would give anything to have a brother like George, but she doesn't say that to Colleen. Instead she says, "Nice room."

Colleen's room is very dark. *Black-lagoonish,* Mica thinks, agreeing with George. A candle with long drips of wax sits on the bedside table. Night-lights provide a dim glow. Colleen flops down on the huge raft of a bed. "Oh, luxury," groans Mica, flopping down on it too.

Colleen fluffs a pillow and stuffs it under her own head. "It's just a bed. You have a bed, don't you?"

"A bunk. And it's hard."

"What do you mean, hard?"

"A bunk on a boat is just a mat with a board under it."

"Ooooh." Colleen is impressed. "Like a prison bed."

"A prison bed?" Mica's never seen a prison bed and wonders how Colleen got to be an expert.

"I read *Tale of Two Cities.*" Colleen rolls onto her stomach and props her chin on her fist. "Are there rats?" She sounds thrilled by the possibility of rats.

"No!" Mica acts indignant, then has to admit, "Well, sometimes—but only when we're at the dock. They climb the mooring ropes and eat our crackers and cereal 'til the Captain traps them. But we haven't had a rat for months."

"Your life is so adventurous…"

Mica is tired of adventure—she'd trade it for a handmade quilt and home-sweet-home pillows any day.

As she lies on her back, Mica stares at the stick-on stars on Colleen's ceiling. They're arranged in patterns, but Mica can't find any familiar constellation. "Where's Orion?" she asks.

"Oh, this isn't an earth sky. This is the sky over Amalana. That's the planet in the trilogy I'm writing."

Mica doesn't know what to say about a fake sky that hovers over a fake planet. "Do they glow in the dark?"

"For a little while."

"They must be phosphorescent."

"Whatever."

Mica could explain phosphorescence, but she knows Colleen wouldn't be interested. She's only good at science because she remembers everything she reads. Instead of explaining phosphorescence, Mica imagines that this is her room and her bed and that the stars are in the right places. "You are so lucky," she whispers.

Colleen sits up and hugs the pillow. "That's a joke, right?"

"No," says Mica, sitting up too. "Your life seems pretty perfect to me."

"Oh yeah. Just perfect." Colleen crushes the pillow against her stomach. "I hate school. School hates me."

"We *both* hate school. It's part of being in the Club of 2. I'm talking about everything else. You have a great family."

"Get to know them."

"What's wrong with them?" Mica hugs her own pillow.

"With George it should be obvious."

"How about your mom?"

Colleen hesitates. "I love my mom, but…"

"But what?"

"I don't know. It's like there was some kind of mix-up." Colleen picks up a framed photo of two little girls that sits behind the drippy candle on the nightstand. The girls are wearing matching polka-dot swimsuits. "This is Mom and Aunt Connie when they were five."

"Which one's your mom?" Mica asks, prepared to like that little girl better.

"I can't tell. Mom can't either. They started out completely identical but Aunt Connie stayed thin and Mom blimped. Aunt Connie won a scholarship and went to college. Mom married her high school boyfriend. Aunt Connie teaches at a major university. Mom..." She pauses, as if hunting for the right words, then gives up. "Mom is just Mom."

"Your mom is the best!" Mica can't believe that Colleen is saying something bad about a mother who has saved a scrap from every piece of clothing her daughter's ever worn. As far as Mica knows, no one has ever saved anything of hers.

"Don't you see?" Colleen whispers. "I don't belong here. I hate the sun. I hate the water." Her nose and both cheeks are peeling. "I despise all the dumb conversations about fish. If my aunt didn't send me books I'd go crazy."

Mica peers around the dark room. Aside from a single window framed by rose-printed curtains, the walls are solid bookshelves, every one of them crammed.

There are books aboard the *Martina*. Most of them are field guides that she and the Captain have studied until the covers have gotten soft and loose—no fiction, though. As Mica runs her eyes along the endless rows of spines, certain words appear over and over. Dragon...sorcerer...wizard...magic. It's kind of embarrassing to think that Colleen takes all this seriously—like she believes in fairies.

"Every book is a door to another world," Colleen says.

"But...they're not real!"

"So?" Colleen bops Mica with her pillow. "Is the real world so great?"

"Well...no." Mica swats Colleen back. "But is a fake one better?"

"Multitudinously!" Colleen's pillow slams Mica on the side of the head, Mica slams back, and for a few minutes the argument turns to squeals as they pummel each other.

Breathing hard, Colleen holds up a hand. "Truce! You can borrow my books if you want. As long as you don't bend down the corners of the pages."

Mica takes a skinny one with a dragon on the cover just to be polite. For a scientist, dragons are irrelevant.

"Good choice!" says Colleen. "The dragons in that series are so empathetic. Read it and we can discuss it. We'll have Club of 2 weekly book discussions."

"Weekly?"

"Or more often if you're a fast reader."

chapter 17

MISS J HAS THE *TALLAHASSEE DEMOCRAT* spread all over the kitchen table. She turns the section she's reading around so Anna can see. "Hey, you think these are our manatees?"

Anna quits doodling in her explorer's notebook. "Gentle giants," she says, reading the caption. "Mother and baby manatee are at home in the Wakulla River." The gentle giants hang still in the water. Anna grins. "They look as lazy as us." It's eleven o'clock and she and Miss J are still in their pajamas.

"We're entitled!" says Miss J. "It's Saturday."

"Saturday," Anna sighs happily. She's not exactly waiting for the mail truck, but every now and then she looks out the window. She's always sure something great will be in the next delivery—and sometimes she's right. A couple of weeks ago Uncle Charles sent a postcard. And last week she got one from Eb, the boy who was her foster brother when she first moved to the neighborhood. All it said was: "Cool hotel! They put free chocolate on your pillow. This postcard was free too. Say hi to everyone." On the front was a picture of a Las Vegas casino. That meant he was definitely with his "fun" mom, not his responsible Aunt Terry.

Miss J looked worried when she read his note. "At least he gets to eat chocolates," Anna said.

Staring at the photo of the glittering neon palace, Miss J just shook her head.

Today Anna's hoping for a letter from Mica. It's been a while—so her friend is sure to write soon. For a second she thinks about Colleen, but then reminds herself that just because Mica has another friend doesn't mean she won't write.

The next time Anna looks out the window, the mail truck is stopped in front of their house. A hand comes out of the truck and stuffs a stack of mail into their box. She only gets a glimpse, but it looks like there's a package curled inside the fliers and magazines.

Anna streaks to the mailbox and grabs the mail—she's right about the package! She's about to streak back when the address on the package catches her eye. Although the return address says Bert's Marina, the handwriting is unfamiliar. Why would someone else be writing to her? What's wrong with Mica?

She forgets for a moment that Ben might skateboard around the corner and see her in her bunny print pajamas. She sits down on the curb and tears the wrapping off. Inside is a letter in the same unfamiliar handwriting and a flower that looks as if it's made out of giant fingernails. The wind riffles the sheet of blue stationery as Anna reads.

Dear Anna,

   As you can tell from the handwriting I'm not Mica.
This is Mica's (honorary) Aunt Emma. If you want, you
can call me that too. Mica will write soon, but at the
moment she won't take her nose out of the fantasy book
she borrowed from her friend Colleen.

   Mica has shared your letters with me and since
you asked about the way adults act, I thought, well, I
know a thing or two about that. So I decided to write
you myself.

   You wondered if an excellent tree climber could
like someone who couldn't make it past the first branch.
To answer that I'm going to tell you a little story. Back
when dinosaurs roamed the earth, I used to love to
dance. I had a boyfriend named Mikey who loved to
dance too. But then I met Bert Floyd, a wonderful guy
who just happened to have two left feet. When I fell in
love with him it was a huge disappointment to the
dancing part of me, but what could I do? Bert was the
one! (You'll understand what I'm talking about when
you get older.)

   I knew my dancing days were over when I married
Bert. Although my knees are creaky, sometimes I still
miss it. Miss J is luckier. If she wants someone to climb
trees with, she has you.

I'm sure Mica will write you a nice long letter soon. In the meantime, here is something I thought you might like, a tarpon scale rose. A church friend of mine makes them to sell in our marina shop. Mica could tell you more about the science of tarpon. All I know is that they get real big and that folks here like to catch them because they put up a good fight.

Ben and Cody caught one while they were here, and it made their whole vacation. Bless their hearts, they released it. If you keep a tarpon, about the only thing you can do is have it stuffed and mounted or make a rose out of its scales. Nobody eats tarpon. My husband says they taste like overgrown sardines. Who would want to eat a hundred-pound sardine?

I thought you might like to put this on the windowsill with your rocks.

Please give my regards to Miss Johnette—I feel like I know her. Tell her about me and dancing. If she really LIKES this Mr. Webster, things will work out even if he never gets past the first branch.

Your new old friend,
Aunt Emma

Anna refolds the sheet of blue stationery. Suddenly, writing a letter about Miss J and Mr. Webster feels sneaky. Anna didn't mean to sneak. She just wanted advice. But if Miss J reads Aunt Emma's note, she'll think that Anna has been complaining about Mr. Webster and even about her. She'll think Anna was going behind her back. Ashamed, she slips the letter into the elastic waist of her pajama bottoms and covers it with the top. Then, holding the rose conspicuously in front of her, she goes back inside.

"It's made of tarpon scales," she says as she sets the rose in her foster mom's hands.

Miss J turns the rose this way and that. "Bet these scales looked a whole lot better on the fish." She turns it over as if it might improve if seen from a different angle. "It's downright ugly," she decides. "But then, I don't like elephant-foot waste-baskets or turtle-shell ash trays either. Things made from animal parts always creep me out. I wonder what the world-famous marine biologist thinks about it." She puts the weird-looking flower down on the counter. "It's a strange thing for Mica to send."

"She didn't send it. Aunt Emma did."

"Hmmm. What did Mica have to say about it in her letter?"

"Mica didn't write. Aunt Emma just sent the rose. I guess she thought I'd like to have it."

"Well, we'd better find a good place for it," Miss J says. "Like behind something."

They end up displaying the tarpon scale rose on a dark shelf in the closet where Edgar the plastic skeleton hangs. "Out of sight, out of mind," says Miss J.

First chance she gets, Anna hides Aunt Emma's letter under the socks in her drawer. Out of sight, out of mind—but not really. Even after it's hidden, Anna can't stop thinking about it. *How could I ever write a letter complaining about Miss J?*

It's early afternoon when they finally get dressed. Miss J says, "We still have plenty of daylight. Let's throw the canoe on the car and plunk it in the water somewhere. What do you say? Salt or fresh?"

"Salt," Anna says, but it's a random choice. She still feels too bad about the letter she wrote to care one way or the other.

They put in near the St. Marks lighthouse and paddle around the brackish water where the St. Marks River empties into Apalachee Bay. "Doesn't that sun feel good?" Miss J asks, drawing in a big lungful of fresh air. "Whoa, look!" She drives her paddle into the muddy bottom with one hand and grabs Beauty's collar with the other. "See that big old gator?"

The spartina grass is thick at the water's edge. It takes Anna a few seconds to pick out the alligator less than five feet away. Its eyes look glazed. Its mouth is open just enough so that she can see the razor-sharp edges of its teeth. "It's sleeping with its eyes open," she whispers.

"Don't let that old boy fool you. A couple of good tail thrashes and he'd be right on top of us. Better hope Beauty doesn't see him. I'll hold her. You back-paddle slowly."

Anna feathers the paddles quietly. The alligator never moves—but it could. It reminds her of the letter lurking at the bottom of her sock drawer, a problem if Miss J ever reads it. She decides that as soon as she gets home she'll throw it away. But by the time they've unloaded the car, heated a frozen pizza, and popped in a video, Anna's forgotten all about it.

So the letter stays hidden.

Waiting.

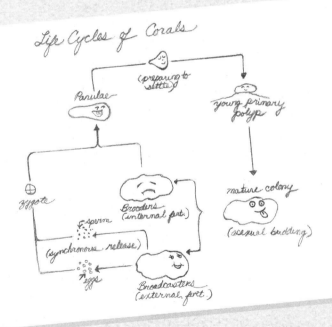

Life Cycles of Corals

chapter 18

"HONEY, I MEAN IT!" Mrs. Farrell exclaims. "You don't need to do the dishes again."

"Yeah, give Leeny a turn," George suggests, a forkful of spaghetti halfway to his mouth.

"It's okay." Mica holds up a dripping glass as if she's inspecting it. "I do *all* the dishes aboard the boat. All the cooking too."

Colleen walks her plate to the sink where Mica stands, up to her elbows in suds, and drops it into the water with a splash. "If you do all the cooking, your dad must be starving."

They're working on a big science project about the life cycles of corals—Mica's choice of topics. It's Mica's third dinner in a row at the Farrells' and her third night of driving Colleen crazy by doing the dishes.

"Last plate, coming up," says George, shoveling the final bite of his third helping of spaghetti into his mouth. He still wears his blue Plantation Fisheries shirt, his name curlicued above the pocket. He still smells like mullet, and his manners are still terrible. "Okay." He tips back in his chair and smiles at Mica. "You may take it away." Even with spaghetti sauce on his chin, even stinking of bait, Mica likes him.

"What a sight," says George as she collects his plate. "A girl helping Ma in the kitchen."

"I don't see *you* helping," Colleen points out.

George pumps up an arm muscle. "Do I look like a girl?" He heaves himself out of the chair and joins his father in front of the TV in the living room.

"It's time to work on our science project," Colleen reminds Mica.

"That's right." Mrs. Farrell rolls up her sleeves. "You girls have work to do. Let me finish here."

But Mica insists on washing everything, even the spoons no one used.

"Although this is incredibly exciting, I'll be in the cave," Colleen announces. "Working on *our* project." And she stomps off.

"We'll finish up quick." Mrs. Farrell reaches for a dish towel.

Mica slides half a step closer to Mrs. Farrell and asks the first question that comes into her head. "What's it like having a twin?"

"Heavens, I can't imagine *not* having a twin. It must be so lonely." And while they finish doing the dishes Mrs. Farrell tells her about growing up as half of something. By the time the work is done, Mica wishes she had a twin too.

"Do you miss her?"

"Oh, yes, terribly. Connie went such a long, long way away to find happiness. I stayed right here." Mrs. Farrell looks around her kitchen. "Connie's the big success, I guess: She teaches at a university, publishes articles, goes to conferences all over the country. But I have my family. That's enough for me."

"In the family department *you're* the big success."

"Well, I guess I am!" She hangs the dish towel on the handle of the stove. "Connie says she's much too busy, but I know deep down she wishes she had a family too. That's why I send Colleen up to stay with her—Connie is my twin, after all."

"Colleen says she's really happy when she's with her aunt."

Mrs. Farrell draws a sharp breath. Mica knows her words hurt her friend's mother. They're like the splinters Mica sometimes gets when she runs down the dock. Pain you don't expect hurts double. But Mrs. Farrell should know that Colleen isn't as loyal as she should be. *If Mrs. Farrell were my mother,* Mica thinks, *I'd never want to go anywhere else.*

"Colleen is more like Connie than she is like me," Mrs. Farrell admits with a sigh. "You know how smart Colleen is— just like Connie. And Connie gives her opportunities that we can't. But oh, how I miss her when she's away."

"I'll be here all summer. I'll come see you."

Mica is imagining sitting down to a meal with the Farrells and no Colleen when large-as-life Colleen sticks her head in the kitchen. "Come *on,* Mica. I got all our sources spread out on the bed."

"In a sec." Mica pulls the plug in the sink. As it empties, she wipes the sides with the sponge. She's drying it carefully when Colleen grabs the paper towel out of her hand and drags her into the cave. "What?" Mica asks as Colleen slams the door.

Colleen is puffing and red-faced. "You know what!"

"No, what?"

"All that, ooh, look at me! I'm so good! I do the dishes and I even dry the sink! Give me a break. Even my mom, the queen of clean, never dries the sink!"

"I just want to help."

"No, you don't. You're taking over and I don't appreciate it!" She points out the open books she's arranged on the bed, but Mica is staring at the poster she worked on for hours: The Life Cycles of Corals. "Faces?" she sputters. "You gave the coral polyps faces?"

"I was bored, okay? Let's get started on this stupid project. We don't have all night."

"Yeah we do. I'm sleeping over."

"But are we really going to work on the project?"

"What else?"

"I don't know," Colleen mumbles, "you might get the urge to vacuum the house or something."

It's Saturday and Emma has had a steady stream of customers all morning. She's giving a tourist with a sunburnt nose advice on catching redfish when Mica calls for a ride—at least that seems to be what she wants. "What are you saying?" Emma covers her free ear with one hand. "I can barely hear you, Mica. Do you want a ride, or don't you?"

"I do," Mica says loudly, then adds in a whisper, "but take your time, okay? George and I are playing Monopoly."

"All right, Mica. I'll be there in about half an hour. Good-bye."

Emma is glad Mica has a friend, but she's beginning to feel like Mica's personal chauffeur. She drove her to the Farrells' after school yesterday. As usual, the Captain was somewhere else. Now she has to fetch her. Mica forgets she has a business to run.

She's still annoyed when she climbs into the van, so she stops at the post office on the way. Vowing to herself that no matter what, she will *not* wait around while Mica uses her "get out of jail free" card, she unlocks the post office box and finds a lumpy package addressed to Aunt Emma Floyd in Anna Casey's handwriting. Mica's name has been omitted. *Guess I'm not the only one who thinks Mica's inconsiderate*, Emma decides.

She opens the package right there on the counter. Out tumbles an ugly piece of rock, wrapped in brown paper. Underneath the rock is a folded note.

Dear Aunt Emma,

Thanks for writing me. Thanks for the rose too—Miss J and I have it on display. Our friend Edgar likes it especially.

I wish I hadn't written about Miss J and Mr. Webster. It sounded like I was complaining about her. I wasn't. Really. Who would complain about the best foster mom ever?

I still don't know whether she LIKES Mr. Webster. If she does I hope she can like both of us at the same time.

Please give this rock to Mica. I don't think you'd want it anyway. It's not very pretty. This is a piece of karst, the limestone under most of north Florida. It's what holds the water in the Floridan aquifer, which is where we get our water. But this isn't any old piece of karst. It's part of a big chunk Miss J and I collected while we were waiting to hear if I would get to stay with her. When we got the yes, we christened it "the Staying Rock." It's always on our kitchen table. I knocked this piece off it for Mica. Maybe it'll give her staying luck too.

Sincerely,
Anna Casey

p.s. Tell Mica that Miss J and I like fantasy books too. Sometimes we take turns reading to each other while we fix supper. One night I said I wish there really were other worlds. She said there are. All you have to do to visit them is put a drop of pond water under a microscope, or gaze at the sky through a telescope. If you look at it that way, who knows how many worlds are going on all around us?

p.p.s. It's all right if Mica is too busy to write me anymore. Tell her I understand.

"Well," says Emma, blinking back tears. "Well, my goodness." She's not sure that Mica deserves a friend like Anna, not the way she's been acting lately. So when she gets out to the van she opens the deep glove compartment and tucks Anna's package and letter inside. She'll show Mica later, sometime when she remembers she has a friend named Anna and she's wishing more than anything that she would hear from her. Today she's putting hotels on Monopoly properties. Anna couldn't be farther from her mind.

Although she swore to herself she wouldn't wait, Emma ends up sipping sweet tea in the kitchen with Mrs. Farrell while Mica bankrupts George in the next room.

"Where is Colleen?" she asks Mrs. Farrell.

"Off somewhere reading. Colleen hates board games."

Emma hears a roar from the living room, then George shoves Mica through the kitchen door. "Take her away! She's cruel and heartless. She stole my last buck!" He pops Mica on the shoulder with his fist. "Get lost, kid!"

Mica pops him back. Emma has never seen a bigger smile on Mica's face. It's only when they're back on US 1 headed for the marina that Emma realizes Mica didn't even say goodbye to Colleen.

chapter 19

MICA SLAPS THE TOP OF EACH piling as she walks down the dock. It's Saturday, but so what? She can't go to Colleen's. Colleen has to visit some stupid cousins in Homestead.

And there's no chance of going to the Farrells' tomorrow either. Tomorrow is Easter, another great big holiday that Mica and the Captain don't celebrate. The Farrells celebrate everything. Even a plain old Sunday is a church-and-family holiday at the Farrells'. She'd thought they might invite her for Easter dinner—she's almost as close as family now.

But not close enough, so she's stuck at the marina for two whole days. She stares out across the basin. Even the flag on the Coast Guard station droops against the flagpole. Nothing is happening anywhere!

In the hot sun the pilings stink of creosote. She used to like the smell, but that was before getting to know the house smells at the Farrells': cookies baking, plug-in air freshener, floor wax.

It seems as if everything has changed since she met the Farrells. It's hard to remember what she used to do before. She hung out with Aunt Emma, sure, but they never really did anything. She worried about her dad a lot—but that wasn't really doing anything either. At the Farrells' they play games, watch

TV (she and George comment on the actors' hairdos and clothes, trying to make each other laugh), they eat Mrs. Farrell's great cooking. But best of all, they talk and talk and talk—except Colleen, who doesn't say much. She's been in a bad mood for days.

Mica's Zodiac rests beside the dock, neglected since her sick day, when it got her in trouble. Mangrove leaves litter the bottom of the little boat. She and her father used to take the Zodiac on expeditions. They'd snorkel and collect specimens. But they haven't done that since she started school. Maybe they can take it out today.

No, bad idea. By the time he wakes up and is what he calls "ambulatory," the tide will be running out. They'd have to fight a stiff current to get down Snake Creek and into the bay, and he'd say that the sun was giving him a headache. Lots of things give him headaches lately.

But isn't there *anything* to do?

She would escape to one of Colleen's alternate worlds, but she finished the latest borrowed book last night. Now she tries to imagine a real life as exciting and world-saving and as full of chances to be brave as Colleen's fantasies.

She's about to let out a death-defying yell and launch off the dock, heroine style, when she remembers. The shorts she has on are her last clean pair—her spare bunk is drowning in dirty laundry. She can't take a chance on getting these dirty too. She doesn't know when the Captain will realize they need to go to the laundromat.

She slaps the last piling. *Might as well see what Aunt Emma is doing.* She trots up the office steps.

But before going inside, Mica stops to look at the shrimp, something she hasn't done in weeks. These are definitely not the same shrimp she observed the last time. Those shrimp took a one-way trip to the reef.

But they might as well be. The shrimp in the tank always do the same things. Today, like every other day, most hang out by the bubbler, enjoying the wiggly sensation of being bounced around on a stream of bubbles. Stealthily Mica lowers a hand through the water. The shiny surface rings her wrist like a bracelet that slides up her arm as her hand dives deeper.

Some of the shrimp twitch away from her, but she scoops up one that hangs dozing on the side of the tank. Instantly its legs scratch against her fingers. She's grabbed a really big one—he'd be king of the shrimp in one of Colleen's books. Still, the two points at the front of its head spread wide; shrimp do that when they're scared.

"Be not afraid," she commands. Water dripping from her elbow, she walks the shrimp to the railing and drops it into the canal. "Go forth. I set you free!" She leans over the railing and watches. For a second the king of the shrimp floats stunned on the surface, easy prey for any predator that might look up. But then it swims slowly to the bottom, where it disappears into the silty turtle grass. "Bo-ring, bo-ring," Mica chants. "Setting free" in the real world isn't as exciting as it is in books.

She dashes into the office yelling, "Hey, Aunt Emma!" but Aunt Emma isn't on her stool. Mica checks the Peg-Board by the door. The key ring is gone. She must be at the post office. "Without me!" That's when Mica realizes that she's gotten all out of sync with Bert's Marina.

While she waits for Aunt Emma to come back, she wipes the counter with an old T-shirt, something that used to be one of her regular jobs. She eats a bag of chips. She's reaching for a second bag when she hears the wheeze of the marina van pulling up out front. The van door slams and Aunt Emma comes in with the mail in her arms. On top is a crinkled sheet of brown paper with a rock balanced in the middle of it.

"Is that from Anna?"

"Good morning, stranger!" Aunt Emma says. "Yes, it is."

"Why did you open my package?" The rock doesn't look much better than the dry leaves Anna sent last time, but that doesn't mean Aunt Emma can go around opening her mail.

"Actually, it's mine and it came a few days ago. I just forgot to bring it inside." Emma sets the wrapping paper and rock on the counter.

"Why did Mica send it to *you?* I'm her friend!"

"She wrote to you about a problem she was having. I thought I could help, so I responded. How long has it been since you wrote to her?"

"I dunno…a while." Thinking back, Mica can't remember. She can't even remember what Anna's problem was—but she still feels hurt that Anna wrote to Aunt Emma instead of to her. She runs a finger over the top of the pitted rock. "Bet you didn't send her anything."

"Yes, I did. A tarpon scale rose."

"Tarpon: *Megalops atlanticus.* Bet you didn't tell her the Latin."

Emma hangs the keys back on the hook. "It must have slipped my mind."

Peeping out from under the rock is a folded sheet of notebook paper: Anna's letter. "Can I see what she wrote?"

"Help yourself." Aunt Emma slides the rock aside.

After reading the letter, Mica folds it up carefully and hands it back. "I don't want to quit writing her. Do you think she *wants* me to?"

"No. She's giving you a way to stop writing if *you* want to. She's being polite."

Mica leans toward Aunt Emma. "What should I do?"

"That's easy." Aunt Emma puts a hand on her cheek. "Write to her."

"I'll write her today." Mica picks up the chunk of karst.

"It's rather ugly, don't you think?" Aunt Emma asks.

Mica studies the holes in the rock. "Not everything has to be pretty. Some things are important in other ways." Anna said in her letter that the karst underlies the whole area where she lives. It holds everything up and it stores the water that she drinks. Not bad for what Aunt Emma calls an ugly rock.

Mica thinks about showing the karst to Colleen, but, like Aunt Emma, all Colleen would see is an ugly rock. She wishes Colleen thought about things the same way Anna does—then instantly unwishes it.

Colleen is my best friend. But even as she says the words inside her head, they don't feel true.

Aunt Emma fluffs the damp hair at the back of her neck. "And now I suppose you want a ride to Colleen's." It's as if she's just seen Colleen pop into Mica's head. "I wish you'd showed up a few minutes earlier when I was going to the post office. It would've saved me a trip."

"I don't want to go to Colleen's. Today I'd rather stay here with you and do—you know—our usual." All of a sudden she misses her old life. But when she goes to sit down, her stool, which always faces Aunt Emma's across the counter, is against the wall behind the rack of sunglasses. "You moved it!"

"You're never here to sit on it. It was kind of in the way."

"No it wasn't!" Mica drags the stool back to its place in front of the counter and flumps down. She props her chin on one hand. "Let's talk." But she can't think of anything to say. They used to talk a lot. But what about?

Aunt Emma is the one who starts the conversation. "How's your father? I haven't spoken to him in a while."

The Captain's aboard the *Martina*, snoring his brains out, but Mica isn't going to tell Aunt Emma that. She swings her legs. "He's fine. Busy with the grant...you know."

"You might remind him that he hasn't paid this month's slip rental. It was due a week ago. It's not like him to be late. He's usually so reliable."

"I'll remind him." Aunt Emma's right. He always remembers stuff like that. But come to think of it, he's forgotten quite a few things lately. He didn't pick her up from school one day last week. She had to call the marina from the school office. When she told Aunt Emma, "Knock on the boat really loud and tell him to come get me," the school secretary had looked at her funny. "He's hard of hearing," Mica had said.

And he forgets to come home until late nearly every evening now. Last night she woke up when she felt the *Martina* list as he clambered aboard. Now she's remembering that the grinning cat clock on the wall of her berth said four twenty-two when the phone rings behind the marina desk.

"Hello?" says Aunt Emma, then her face breaks into a big smile. She covers the receiver with her hand. "It's my grandsons!" Aunt Emma spends a month with Alex and Damon every summer when school gets out. "I'll be there before you know it!" she says to whichever boy is on.

Mica stays on her stool, but she isn't really listening. She wonders if her father is eating enough. She hasn't cooked for him much lately. When the Captain picks her up after school on his moped, she usually asks him to drop her off at the Farrells' so she and Colleen can do homework together. Most of the time they invite her to stay for dinner. Mr. Farrell drives her home, but he doesn't know her father is never at the boat when he drops her off. Mica doesn't tell him that the Captain is at the bar across the creek. She figures that her dad turns in there after delivering her to Colleen's and drinks instead of fixing himself supper. She never finds a dirty dish or an open can when she gets home.

And she's noticed that he doesn't go out on the water anymore, doesn't collect specimens. That could be because he goes out with Dr. Winn and keeps the specimens at the lab. But the tanks on the picnic table are green with algae—she dumped the last damselfish in the canal last week. She's not even sure how often her father works. But she is sure of one thing. He's drinking again.

Mica carefully picks up the karst. "Think I'll show my dad the rock."

Aunt Emma covers the receiver again. "Write Anna back, okay?"

"I will."

"Send her a chunk of what the Keys are built on—whatever that is." She goes back to groaning over one of the boy's latest knock-knock jokes.

As Mica walks back down the dock, a bright red powerboat with twin diesels loafs into the canal. She could trot back and pump the guy's gas, but suddenly it seems urgent that she check on her dad. Maybe she *has* ignored him lately, but not today.

She'll start by brewing him coffee so strong the smell will levitate him from his berth in the aft cabin. She'll fry bacon and eggs; he'll eat every bite.

She's so busy thinking about all the things she's going to do for him that when she slides the hatch and climbs down, she lets out a startled yelp.

"Don't worry," the Captain croaks. "I'm more alive than I look."

She sets down the chunk of karst on top of the refrigerator and falls into the dinette seat opposite him. He looks groggy and gray and sunken-in. His spine is as bent as a fishhook. He seems even skinnier than he did the last time she really looked at him—which was when? Definitely before Colleen.

"Captain, get ready for a treat!" She pretends she doesn't see that the hand he runs through his thinning hair is shaking. "I'm fixing you breakfast."

"Hold the breakfast. Just make coffee."

"Coming right up!" Once he's had a cup, she'll offer breakfast again. She's measuring the coffee when she notices that the Captain has picked up Colleen's book and is looking at the jacket. "It's a good story," she says. "I bet you'd like it."

"I don't think so. Flying horses?"

"Just imagine that evolution turned out different. It *could* have."

"Flying horses that talk?"

"We talk, why not horses?" She remembers Anna and Miss J reading aloud. "I know, we can read it to each other. We'll take turns."

"Would this be in place of the father-daughter puzzle?" Then he looks around, surprised. "Speaking of the dreaded jigsaw, where'd it go?"

"I threw it overboard a long time ago. The fish are working on it."

"Funny, I never noticed." For a moment he covers his eyes with his hand, but then he opens the book and turns to the first page. "All right. Talking horses might be entertaining. I'll read, you make that coffee so stiff you can stand a spoon up in it, okay?" He begins to read the first chapter of *The Magic Horses of*

Orana aloud. She likes hearing him read. Without even knowing it, she's missed the sound of his voice.

He's still reading the first chapter, the coffee *drip-dripping* through the coffeemaker, when Aunt Emma's face appears at the screen window by the dinette. "Mica?" The screen goes dark as she puts her face up to it and shades her eyes. "Colleen's on the phone," she says. "One of her cousins stepped on a broken bottle. They took him to the emergency room for stitches, so her family came home. She wants to know if you can come over."

Mica has just selected the perfect mug for her father's coffee, but she sets it down on the counter with a clatter. "Tell her I said yes!"

As Aunt Emma scuffs back down the dock, Mica turns to her father. "It's okay if I go, isn't it? Tomorrow, when it's Easter at the Farrells', we'll spend the day together. We'll read and go out in the Zodiac." She gives the Captain her most pleading look. "This is my only chance to see Colleen for the whole, whole weekend. You'll ride me over, won't you, please?"

"So much for talking horses." He flips the cover shut.

"Can we go now?"

"May I drink my coffee first?"

"Yes. Of course." She fills the mug—not too full—and sets it in front of him, then parks her butt at the very edge of the bench opposite him. "Is it too hot? I could blow on it."

Mica jumps out of Mr. Farrell's rusted pickup and slams the door. "Bye. And thanks again for the ride home."

"You have a great Easter, young lady," he calls as she trots across the marina parking lot toward the dock.

"You too, sir," she calls back. The egg carton in the plastic bag swinging on her arm is full of colored eggs. Her favorite is the one George dyed for her. After one minute in each of the five dyes it turned the color of dry asphalt. George christened it the "death egg."

In return she gave him her bluest blue egg. It sat in the dye the whole time they were decorating the other eggs. Colleen complained that she was hogging that color, but the egg came out Gulf Stream blue. George pronounced it almost as impressive as the sinister death egg.

But while they sat at the kitchen table splashing dye and laughing, Mica kept wondering what the Captain was doing. Where had he gone after he dropped her off, back to bed, or to the bar?

She probably could've weaseled her way into a dinner invitation, but she knew that while she was eating Mrs. Farrell's smothered pork chops the Captain would be eating canned food by himself—if he ate at all. So she asked for a ride home. She and her dad will eat canned food together.

But the first thing she notices as she walks toward the boat is that no moped rests against the piling. The only thing resting is a herring gull that has settled on top of the piling, bill tucked down into its chest for the night.

Aboard the empty boat, Mica arranges the dozen colored eggs in a plastic bowl and centers it on the dinette so the Captain can see them when he comes home—she'll have to explain George's death egg.

She goes through the canned goods looking for something special, but there isn't much to choose from. Cream of chicken and tomato bisque soup mixed together might be good, especially if she adds a box of macaroni. Trying to decide whether she needs to boil the noodles first or throw them in the soup as is, she sets the noodle box and the two cans on the table. Since she doesn't know when he'll get there, she doesn't open anything.

The karst from Anna sits on top of the refrigerator looking as dull as the death egg, which gives her an idea. While she waits, she'll write to Anna.

The sun is just melting into the bay when Mica trudges up to the parking lot. In the orange light the scattered broken coral seems to glow. Mica moves the chunks around with her big toe, hunting until she finds the best piece. *Bet Mrs. Farrell's pork chops were good,* she thinks. But her cream of chicken tomato noodle soup will be good too.

Maybe by the time she finishes the letter to Anna the Captain will be home to eat it.

Dear Anna,

Sorry I didn't write you. I <u>don't</u> want to stop writing.
(I'll try to do better.) Thanks for the karst. Aunt
Emma thought it was ugly—but what does she know?
She thinks tarpon scale roses are beautiful. No offense
if you liked the one she sent, but I bet you didn't.

Tomorrow (Easter to everyone but us) my father and I
will put the karst under the dissecting scope and check
it out. After that we'll go out in my Zodiac and
snorkel. It will be our own private holiday. It won't be
Easter. It will be Father-Daughter Nature Day.

I couldn't think of what to send you, then I
remembered that Aunt Emma said I should send you a
piece of what the islands of the Keys are made of,
which is fossilized coral. I didn't have to go far for
that. Chunks of it are scattered all over the parking
lot. You can tell it's fossilized because it sparkles.
There's so little dirt around here that Aunt Emma buys
topsoil in bags to keep the flower garden in front of
the office going. The closest we have to dirt is marl,

which is whitish and powdery. As soon as it gets wet it turns slick as ice. Put your foot on wet marl and before you know it, you put your butt on wet marl!

I wish you could come with the Captain and me on our Nature Day. Too bad we don't live closer together.

Your sorta sister,
Mica

chapter 20

JOHNETTE RAPS ON ANNA'S DOOR. When there's no answer she
sings out, "Laundry delivery!" and bumps the door open with
her hip. Anna must be in the bathroom. The shower is running.

Johnette sets the laundry basket down on the bed. Over the
sound of running water, she hears a voice from the bathroom.
"Hold still and let me soap your ear." Anna couldn't be giving
the dog a shower, could she? Actually that's not so far-fetched.
Maybe she's giving Beauty a makeover with the gift from
Johnette's mother. Knowing that her daughter would never buy
Anna anything as frivolous as fancy toiletries, Johnette's mom
sent Anna a gift box of body sprays, shower gels, and lotions.
Anna was thrilled when she got home from school and found it.
Leave it to Anna to use the gift on Beauty instead of herself.

Johnette pulls a dresser drawer open. She's stuffing in gym
socks when she sees the edge of a letter signed "Aunt Emma."
*Guess Anna was too distracted by the fish scale rose to mention the let-
ter,* Johnette thinks. She wouldn't mind knowing what Aunt
Emma has to say about that ugly rose, so she pulls the sheet of
blue paper out of the drawer, sits on the edge of Anna's bed, and
begins to read.

But the letter isn't about the rose. It's a letter of advice about her and Jonah Webster. Why would Emma Floyd be advising Anna about something like that?

Anna must have written to her about us. Why didn't she just ask me if she had questions?

Then Johnette remembers some of the things she's said to Anna about Jonah. We're not dating. He's just a friend. Which isn't the whole truth. Heck, it isn't even half the truth. She's crazy about the man. But Johnette is not the kind of person who gets all fluttery about guys. Better to keep quiet about it and just see what happens. But how has keeping quiet affected Anna?

Johnette folds the letter and puts it in her lap. *My goodness,* she thinks. *What have I done?* It's not hard to figure out that since Anna isn't sure what's going on, she's scared. Johnette had thought that things were fine and there was no need to talk about her and Mr. Webster. But she realizes now that not telling Anna what's going on is its own kind of lie—and Anna's been lied to before.

How many people have been less than truthful with Anna? Johnette feels her cheeks burn. How many decisions in the girl's life have been made without consulting her? And it's not like the boyfriend thing hasn't been a problem for Anna before. Her first foster mother gave her up when she decided to get married.

Johnette has wondered why Anna seems sad lately. She's blamed it on lack of friends, being new at school, missing her real family. She's blamed everything but herself. Now Johnette is mortified. *I just won't see him,* she decides. *Let Jonah Webster sit on the back burner for as long as it takes to reassure Anna.* Thinking about telling him she can't see him anymore, she has a hard time breathing. But too bad. Anna comes first. Johnette gets a funny feeling in the middle of her chest and wonders if this is what it feels like when your heart breaks. *Serves you right,* she tells herself. *You were way too busy thinking about yourself.*

She hasn't heard the shower turn off or the thumping in the bathroom as Anna dries the dog.

"Miss J?" Anna stands in the open bathroom door in jeans and a soaked T-shirt, her draggled dog at her side. She stares at the letter in Johnette's lap and looks terrified. "Miss J...I never meant...I'm so, so sorry!"

Johnette jumps up from the bed, sending the letter wheeling to the floor. "No, Anna." She throws her arms around the girl. "I'm the one who's sorry. I should have talked all this over with you a long time ago. Don't worry about Jonah. We'll just give that whole thing a rest. It'll just be the two of us again." The words feel right when she says them to Anna. But she knows that it will be different when she says them to him, which will be real soon. He'll come over when he gets off work.

Holding Anna, she wonders how it is possible to be this happy and this sad at the same time. She has the daughter she's always wanted, but she may have to give up Jonah, the guy she'd always waited for and had long ago given up on finding.

"No," Anna says quietly, pushing away from her.

Johnette brushes back Anna's long bangs so she can really see her blue eyes. "No?"

"No. You can't do that. It's not fair to Mr. Webster. He loves you as much as I do...and you love him."

"Shoot. I guess I do," Johnette says, surprised. She's never let herself think it before, let alone say it, but she does love him. She puts her hands on Anna's shoulders. "I love both of you."

"Well...duh!" Anna smiles, showing her chipped front tooth. "Good thing you have a big heart."

"Big heart, big everything!" They're laughing when there's a knock at the front door. "What do you say? Should we let him in?"

Anna nods solemnly.

"Hey, over here!"

The bedsprings *quinge* as Anna sits up. "Cody!"

This time he's wiggled the window up and his whole head is inside.

"Cody, I *told* you… You can't go around sticking your head in girls' windows."

Beauty lets out a short bark, then jumps down and walks to the window, tail wagging.

"Why not?" Cody's arm joins his head inside her room. He moves a couple of Anna's rocks and folds his arms on the windowsill. "You're still not naked." With the sun hitting the back of his neck, the skin over his ears looks awfully white. He must've just had a haircut. "Hey, new rock!" he exclaims, holding up the latest addition to Anna's collection.

"Mica sent it. It's fossilized coral."

"I have some too. It's all over the parking lot at Uncle Bert's marina."

"I know, Mica told me." She throws herself back down on her stomach across the bed.

"I saw Miss J drive off with Mr. Webster. Where are they going? Someplace you're not 'lowed?"

"He's taking her out for ice cream," Anna says into the pillow. It was her idea. She sat the two of them down on the sofa and told them they should go out for dinner. Miss J said they couldn't possibly. For one thing, that would mean leaving Anna alone after dark. Mr. Webster, who had no idea he had almost been dumped, pointed out that Anna is old enough to babysit, so she should certainly be able to take care of herself for a couple of hours, but Miss J was afraid that something would happen. They settled for a daylight date to Cold Stone Creamery on Tennessee Street. "I'll bring you something back," Miss J told her.

Mr. Webster looked incredibly happy to be going somewhere with just Miss J. "Thanks," he'd whispered to Anna as they headed for the door. "I owe you."

Anna just has to trust that sharing Miss J will be all right. She remembers Miss J's big heart.

"Don't you like ice cream?" Cody asks, boosting himself up so his stomach is on the windowsill.

"Of course I do, but it's a date. You don't take a kid on a date."

"I know. Ben and Cass never take me. But why are you just lying there?"

"I'm thinking."

"About what?"

"Things."

"I'll think with you," he says, sliding the rest of the way into the room and falling on the floor. "Ow!" He rubs his elbow. "Two heads are better than one."

"There were already two heads in this room."

"Dog heads don't count." Beauty gets up on her back legs and puts her paws on his shoulders. She licks his chin. He scratches her ear. "Why is Beauty wet? Hey, do you have any soda?"

"Miss J always has soda."

"I know. I was being polite."

"You doof!" she says, getting off the bed. She walks over to him and gives his head a quick rub, his short hair bristling against her palm. "Would you like brownies with that soda?"

"*Would I!* I mean, yes, please. That would be extremely agreeable."

They sit side by side on the sofa with their feet on the coffee table. "Gross!" says Anna when Cody belches for, like, the ninety-ninth time.

"Had to! My dad says it's dangerous to hold it in."

Anna wonders if she'll have to put up with that kind of guy-thinking if Mr. Webster becomes permanent.

Cody belches for the hundredth time, then laughs. They've consumed soda and brownies until both of them feel a little sick.

"Maybe we should throw a ball or something," Cody suggests. "You know, work the sugar off so we have room for supper."

Anna wonders if Mr. Webster will be eating supper with them—and if he'll show up again on Saturday and Sunday. Maybe it's selfish, but she still wants time alone with Miss J.

"Come on," says Cody. "Let's go outside."

But Anna has seen Cass and Jemmie jog past the front window three times since she and Cody parked on the sofa. The girls are on the track team, both serious runners. They'll be circling the block every few minutes until they get yelled home for supper. Anna's tired of sitting there, but she doesn't want to risk being seen with Cody. "Let's climb our tree instead."

"Sure!"

Calling it "our tree" really works on Cody. It's like the magic phrase that makes hypnotized people do the hypnotist's will.

Even though they probably have a few minutes before Cass and Jemmie pass by again, Anna would rather not take a chance. She grabs Cody's arm before he can dash out the front door. "You have to go back out the same way you came in."

His eyes widen. "Through your bedroom window?"

"It's bad luck to come in and go out different ways." She didn't make this up. Aunt Eva, who was very superstitious, told her that several times.

Anna follows Cody back to her room and watches as he drops from the sill. He's up to his ankles in the ferns when she steps up on the windowsill. "What're you doing?" he asks.

"Coming out."

"You got *into* your room through the window?"

Anna hates to lie, but she can't tell him the real reason they're jumping out the window. "Sure," she says. "I do it all the time."

"Cool!"

The *thump* she makes landing in the ferns is followed closely by another *thump* as Beauty lands beside her. Anna and her dog take off running for the Old Senator.

"Hey, wait for me!" Cody catches up with them just as they reach the tree.

Anna and Cody are at the top of the ladder when Anna hears the pingy slap of sneakers on the pavement in front of the house. Sitting on the first branch, they're hidden by the house. "Let's stay here," she says. "It's the most comfortable."

"Thought we were gonna climb."

"Let's just rest a minute so we can digest. You don't want to get a cramp."

"That's stupid. Climbing isn't like swimming. Is it?" But his skinny back curves as he slumps on the branch, settling into a comfortable digesting position. "You know, with this haircut I can feel the wind all over my head."

Anna lifts her hair off the back of her neck and holds it up so she can feel the wind too.

They're still on the lowest branch, feeling the wind, when they hear the next round of running footsteps—more than two this time. "Come on!" a boy shouts. "Let's hit the school, shoot a few hoops."

"Sounds like Ben," Cody whispers.

"You boys want your butts whipped, it's okay with us!"

"And that's Jemmie," Cody says. "If we hurry we can catch up!" His slumped spine straightens and he lowers a sneaker to the first rung.

"No, Cody!" Anna hooks a finger through the belt loop on his jeans. "We're going to do something way better."

"Like what?"

"Like...well..." Anna thinks fast. "Today we're climbing to the highest branch."

Cody gazes into the crown of the tree. He blinks twice. "I don't think I can."

"You can if I help you."

"Well...okay."

Sometimes Anna has to boost Cody up. Sometimes she hangs belly-down on the branch over his head, her arms dangling, and pulls him up.

Cody is scared at first, but each time he makes it safely to a higher branch he gets cockier. "Bet Ben couldn't climb this high." They are looking down on the roof, which is beginning to turn pinkish as the sun sinks into the trees.

"I bet he couldn't," she agrees, "but don't tell him *you* did it. He'd never let you do it again."

"I won't. He always thinks he's the boss of me. This is *our* secret."

There's no need to go any higher. By now the kids have been at Monroe Middle a good twenty minutes. Cass and Jemmie are probably whipping the guys' butts. Those girls are good. Anna knows because during the summer they'd let her play on the girls' side a few times, but she'd always felt like the weak link.

Without her the girls are probably beating them bad. It won't be long before the boys point out that it's got to be almost suppertime. They'll say something lame-o about how they let the girls win, and then they'll head back this way. It's time to get out of the tree because up this high they are definitely visible from the street. "This is it!" Anna announces. "Highest branch!"

"Nuh-uh. If we were on the highest branch, our heads would stick out the top of the tree."

"This counts as the highest branch because it's the highest one that will support us. They're too skinny at the top."

Cody tips his head back, resting it against the trunk. "That branch isn't skinny," he says, pointing. "I think *that's* the highest."

"I dunno, Cody. It looks like it might be dead."

"It still has leaves on it."

"Not many. It's *almost* dead."

"I'm going to climb up there before it gets *all* the way dead. And see, there's a nest up there. I'm going to get it. You wait here."

Mr. Webster's pickup rounds the corner in front of the house. "Look, Cody. The date's over. Forget the nest. Miss J brought me an ice cream. We can share."

But Cody pulls his feet up under him and rests both sneaker soles on the branch. He creeps a hand up the trunk, concentrating powerfully on the branch over his head. "You can't jump, Cody. You're too little."

He spits on his palms.

"I mean it, Cody. Don't you dare jump."

As the last word leaves her mouth, the boy's knees pump and he pushes off with both feet. The slap of his palms on the branch is instantly followed by a loud *crack*.

A sneaker smashes into her shoulder. She throws an arm around the trunk and stares at him falling and falling. She hears someone yell in the front yard, but she can't turn her head to see who it is. She can only watch Cody shrink as the distance between them grows.

The fall is slowed as he *whumps* into branches. He's still holding the broken limb in his hands but it's breaking to bits as it encounters the tangle of healthy branches. His eyes, wide open, stare up at her. All of a sudden he drops the dead branch and somehow manages to catch another limb with one hand. He swings like that, safe, she thinks, but only for a second. His fingers slip.

There are no more branches to slow him, nothing to hang onto. He falls the last ten feet and lands flat on his back next to Beauty.

The dog lets out a startled yelp, then streaks across the yard. She passes two people who are streaking even faster toward the Old Senator. Anna knows it's Miss J and Mr. Webster, but she can't look at them, because all she can see is Cody lying on the ground, not moving. His eyes aren't open anymore.

Then she sees the top of Mr. Webster's head, Miss J's ponytail flying straight behind her as she catches up with him. "No!" he warns. He puts a hand on her shoulder. "Don't move him. Call 911." Miss J runs for the house.

The coins in Mr. Webster's pockets jingle when he falls to his knees. As she lets herself down from branch to branch, Anna can hear him talking to Cody. "Hang in there, Cody. Help is coming. Stick with me now." She wonders why Cody doesn't answer, why he doesn't move at all—and she wonders if Miss J knows about the bald spot at the back of Mr. Webster's head—and then she wonders if she's a really bad person for noticing a bald spot when Cody is lying so still. But nothing feels as real as it did a few seconds ago. The air seems thick. It slows her down the way it would in a dream.

She's at the top of the ladder looking down. "Is he hurt?" she says softly.

Mr. Webster looks up. "I think he'll be okay."

A faint cry drifts over the house. "Co-dy! Be-en!" Mrs. Floyd is calling the boys home for supper. Anna half expects Cody to jump up, dust himself off, and run home, but he doesn't.

"Bo-oys!" Mrs. Floyd's voice is joined by the distant wail of a siren.

Anna hurries down the ladder and kneels on the ground next to Cody. "Mr. Webster?" The man puts a finger to his lips, then bends down close to Cody and listens to him breathe. "Look!" Anna points out. "The back of his head is bleeding."

"Probably just a small cut. Scalps bleed like crazy." But Mr. Webster's face is as white as notebook paper. "I bet the fall just knocked the wind out of him. The paramedics will fix him up. Run to the street and flag them down."

She reaches the front yard just as the ambulance brakes hard in front of Miss J's house. Its siren and wheeling light bring the neighbors out into the street.

"Lord, lord," moans Jemmie's grandmother as the medics carry Cody around the side of the house on a stretcher.

The kids, just back from shooting hoops, stop a couple of houses away, confused. Ben drops the ball and sprints down the street. "Cody!" They all swarm the ambulance.

Anna feels Mr. Webster's hand on her shoulder.

"It's my fault," says Miss J, walking over to them. "What kind of mother encourages kids to climb trees?"

"Accidents happen." Mr. Webster puts an arm around her shoulders, and with his other hand he gently pulls Anna back against him. The three of them support each other like tent poles.

chapter 21

MICA IS SITTING SO FAR FORWARD her knees touch the dashboard. "We're not going anywhere until you buckle that seatbelt." Emma watches until the belt is tight across the girl's chest.

"Okay," says Mica. "Can we go now?"

Taking her time starting the van, Emma wonders why Mica is always so desperate to get to the Farrells'. It doesn't seem quite healthy. "Isn't this a little early to be going to Colleen's? Those poor people are probably still in bed."

"She said to come early."

"*This* early?" Emma adjusts the rearview mirror. "I wonder how Anna's doing. We haven't heard a thing from her in a while." This is her way of asking whether Mica sent the girl a letter.

"I wrote last. I sent her some fossilized coral. The Captain mailed it." Mica rests her flip-flops on the backpack at her feet.

Emma feels better on two counts: For one thing, Mica isn't so Colleen-crazy that she forgot all about her friend in Tallahassee. And for another, the Captain pulled himself together, at least long enough to mail a letter. Small blessings, but Emma counts them.

She pulls out of the parking lot onto the empty highway. An empty road on a Saturday morning at the height of tourist season

218

shows just how early it is. "I wonder why Anna hasn't written back. I hope she's all right."

"She's probably just busy." Mica sticks an arm out the window. "The air would be breezier if you drove faster."

"We could stop at the post office on our way," Emma suggests, "and see if there's anything from Tallahassee."

But that puts Mica into a panic. "I *have* to get to Colleen's. We're going to the library to work on our project."

"The library doesn't open until ten o'clock on Saturdays."

"I know, but we have to do other things too."

Emma goes back to worrying. Are things so bad at home that Mica has to escape to Colleen's? She frowns. "I just remembered, your father still hasn't paid the slip rental. If he waits much longer he'll be a full month behind."

"My fault!" Mica slides down in her seat, straining the seatbelt, and forces the fingers of her right hand into the pocket of her shorts. "He gave me the check last week." Her hand comes back out of the pocket—and so does the check, in stiff little lumps. "I guess I washed it."

"Just get your father to write me another one. Soon, okay?" Actually Emma's relieved. At least the check got written. Lately she's been very concerned about Dr. Delano. Bert calls her a worrywart, but she has good reason to worry this time. She's a light sleeper. She knows how late Mica's father comes home from the bar, and she can guess the state he's in. Two nights ago he lumbered past their houseboat rapping his knuckles on the wall, *thump, thump, thump.* Even Bert woke up. "If he does that again," he said, "he can find another place to park his boat."

She wonders for the umpteenth time if she should tell someone about Mica's father. So far, though, she hasn't been able to bring herself to do it. If she reported him for neglect, the state would have every reason to take Mica away—and that's what stops her. All the Delanos really have is each other.

Mica pops her seatbelt as they roll into the yard. "Hi!" she yells out the window. Mrs. Farrell, who's kneeling in her garden, waves a gloved hand. The van has barely come to a stop when Mica jumps out and trots over to the flowerbed. She dumps her pack by a jasmine bush.

"Don't forget to say good-bye to your aunt."

"Bye, Aunt Emma. Have a great day! Sell lots of bait!" Mica doesn't even hear the van grind out over the pea gravel in the driveway. She's already on her knees beside Colleen's mother.

"You don't have to help me—I actually like pulling weeds. Go on inside. I'm afraid you'll have to wake up Colleen. We weren't expecting you for another hour."

"Sorry. This was the only time Aunt Emma could bring me." Mica throws a clump of Spanish needles on the pile. "I'll help you 'til Colleen gets up."

They kneel side by side, wrenching out weeds. "Warm already, isn't it?" says Mrs. Farrell, blotting her forehead with the back of her gardening glove. She's glowing with perspiration.

"Roasting," Mica agrees. She doesn't actually feel hot, but she wants to be sympathetic.

Mica has forgotten all about Colleen when her friend stumbles out of the house. Her hair is pushed up on one side. She looks bad. "Mica! What're you doing out here?" Her mood is bad too.

"Aunt Emma had to drive me over early." Mica gives her a sincere smile.

Colleen opens the door a little wider. "Get in here."

Mica hesitates. She'd rather stay outside with Colleen's mom.

"Go on," Mrs. Farrell urges. "I made cinnamon buns this morning."

Mica gives in when she hears the words "cinnamon buns." Mrs. Farrell makes the stickiest, gooiest, best cinnamon buns in the world. Even though there's no oven aboard the *Martina*, Mica asked her for the recipe. She taped it on the wall over her bunk beside all the photos.

Colleen's brother is at the kitchen table, smoking a cigarette and reading the fishing report in the *Keynoter*. "Well, if it isn't honorable sister number two." He presses his hands together and executes a bow in his chair. "Greetings, Mica."

"Well, if it isn't honorable brother number one," she answers, returning the bow before falling into the chair next to him. "Greetings, George."

"I believe these are yours." He picks up and presents the plate of buns with a sweeping gesture. "Mom made these especially for you."

"She did?"

"Sure. Unlike some girls I could name, you don't take them for granted."

Colleen sticks her tongue out at him.

The best way to eat Mrs. Farrell's cinnamon buns is to unwind the long spiral of dough—Mica learned that from Colleen—but as soon as she starts unrolling one, Colleen makes a point of cutting her own into dainty pieces with a knife. She then eats the segments one at a time with a fork.

"Wow," says George. "What's up with you, Leeny? A sudden attack of manners?"

"Shut up," says Colleen. "And quit calling me Leeny."

Mica eats the first bun in a long dangling spiral, but cuts the second one into small bites like Colleen.

George fakes a shiver. "Ladies, ladies, your manners are giving me the creeps."

Mica sticks her pinkie in the air when she picks up her cup of juice—she saw a table of wealthy women sip tea that way once when she went with the Captain to a fundraiser for sea turtles. Nose in the air, she takes a tiny sip and dabs at the corners of her mouth with her napkin.

George tips back in his chair and guffaws. "Well, lah-dee-dah!"

Mica beams.

Colleen shoves her chair back suddenly. "Let's go," she says.

"Shouldn't we do the dishes?"

Colleen widens her pale blue eyes. "Go ahead. Give George a heart attack!"

"Mica doing the dishes wouldn't give me a heart attack. She's the good daughter. But if *you* did them? Now *that* would put me six feet under."

"Ha. Ha." Colleen pushes her chair in hard enough to slosh George's coffee all over his newspaper. Mica blots it with a paper napkin, then trots after Colleen.

The only sound as they walk to the library is the monotonous conversation of their flip-flops slapping their heels. "You mad?" Mica finally asks.

Colleen keeps trudging.

Mica steps in front of her and walks backwards. "Are you?"

Colleen stares at her from under her startling white eyelashes. "Quit trying to take over my family, okay?"

Mica feels as if she's just been slapped. "Sorry," she mumbles, turning around again and watching the ground.

"I mean, jeez, Mica. You have a family. You don't have to steal mine."

"I'm not trying to steal yours. And anyway, I never had a brother."

"Brothers are not the best deal. Seriously. George makes fun of me all the time. My books, my room, everything I do. He insists on calling me Leeny—which I think is his sick idea of a fat joke. And he stinks up the bathroom."

They look both ways, then jog across US 1, their packs bumping their backs. "In fact," Colleen gasps, winded from the short sprint, "you can take George if you want. I am *so* over having a brother."

Mica grins as they walk up the gravel drive to the library. "Okay, I'll take him."

"Good. When we get back to my house we'll put him in a big trash bag and throw him in the back of Dad's truck."

"How about your mom? Can I have her too?"

Colleen's head whips around. "No! You have your own mother." She stops at the foot of the library steps. "I mean, you do, don't you? You never talk about her."

Mica stares at the lacy shade cast on the concrete steps by a royal poinciana. "What?" says Colleen. "What's the matter?"

Mica is trying to pick out one of the many stories she's told before. *My mother is a famous ballet dancer who is touring Europe.* That's the one she told Ben and Cody. *My mother is in the witness protection program…she's a movie actress…she's with the circus…she's climbing Mount Everest.*

But if Mica wants Colleen to share her mother the story has to be sad, heartbreaking even. The real story of how Mica's mom walked out and left them is sad; it's the one she hates the most. But is it dramatic enough? For once Mica decides that even if it isn't dramatic, the truth is the right story. Her friend deserves the truth.

She sits down on the library steps and slumps against the metal book drop box. It's hard to begin. "You've got to promise...," she starts.

But Colleen is already nodding. "You know I'm not going to tell."

Mica eases the chain out from inside her shirt, her heart racing. She separates the ring from the shower key and the charm. "See this?" The gold band on the chain turns slowly.

"A wedding ring! Whose?"

"My mom's."

Colleen slaps both hands over her mouth, then lowers them and whispers, "Is she dead?"

Mica blinks. She lets out the breath she was going to use to start the real story. She thinks fast. A dead mother would be heartbreaking for sure. Much sadder than the truth. Colleen would *have* to share her family after hearing a story like that.

This time she swoons against the book drop so dramatically it lets out a dull *clang*—and the truth blows away like Anna's milkweed seeds. "We got caught in a storm," she stage-whispers. "Our mast snapped. My father tried to save her, but she washed overboard."

Colleen's cheeks look even pinker than usual. "Was she...?" Colleen whispers back.

Mica nods gravely. "Her body was never found." Mica can get tears in her eyes when she wants to—in fact, she had sort of planned on it. But the tears in her eyes now are hotter than the ones she makes up; they come from deeper in.

She turns away from Colleen, confused. She can't possibly be crying over a dead mother. Her mother isn't dead. But she doesn't know who she's crying for. Her dad? Herself? All she knows is that she can't stop. Through her tears the dazzle of red poinciana flowers and lacy green leaves shifts like a bright curtain. She tries to blink the tears back in, but she can't. She wraps her arms around herself so tightly that her fingers almost touch in back. She lowers her forehead to her knees. Her tears soak the legs of her shorts.

"Come on, Mica, don't cry. It's not *that* bad." Colleen gives Mica's back a quick pat. "Parents get killed all the time in books. The kids are sad at first, but things usually turn out okay for them. Sometimes better."

"Only in books!" Mica chokes out. Snot is running down her throat and it hurts to take a deep breath. "There aren't any magic doors in real life. Everyone is just stuck with whatever life they have!"

"I know," Colleen says quietly. She bumps Mica's shoulder with hers. "Guess that means *I'm* stuck with George, huh? *I'm* the one who should be crying!" Colleen stands up and tugs her shorts away from the backs of her legs. "It's hot out here. Let's go inside and see if we can get online. I want to e-mail Aunt Connie."

Mica is swallowing hard, trying to make the thick feeling in her throat go away, when Colleen opens the library door. "Ah, air conditioning," Colleen sighs. Mica staggers after her. Colleen looks back over her shoulder. "All right," she whispers loudly. "You can share my family. But with rules."

"What rules?"

"First, you have to quit helping Mom. She *likes* doing all the stuff around the house. It's her reason for living." Colleen glances toward the librarian on duty, waves. "Hi, Miss Bell." She goes back to her low voice. "And don't laugh at George's jokes. They're not funny."

"I was being polite."

"No, you were sucking up."

"Okay. I won't laugh." But Mica wonders how she'll get them to really, really like her if she treats them the way Colleen does.

They have to love Colleen. They don't have to love her.

Colleen e-mails Aunt Connie, then messes around on the Internet the rest of the morning. Mica does their report; it seems to be part of the trade for sharing her family.

After a couple of hours, Mica insists they take a break. Colleen wants to stay where it's cool but Mica says, "I'll show you another kind of cool." And she leads Colleen across the simmering parking lot to the little park behind the library. It's on the bay side of the island with a tiny strip of sandy beach and lots of mangroves in the shallow water. A breeze is blowing. Mica kicks her turquoise flip-flops into the air and wades in. "Come on!"

But when she turns around, Colleen is sitting on a swing pushing herself back and forth with the toes of her flip-flops, never getting the least bit airborne. "This isn't cool," Colleen complains.

Sheepshead minnows swirl around Mica's ankles like an underwater wind. "You'd be cool if you were in the water!"

"I don't *do* saltwater."

"You did when you visited the marina."

Still holding the chains of the swing, Colleen lifts one pinkie in the air. "I was just being polite."

Mica ignores the hint of meanness and wades in a little deeper. She digs her toes into the sand and sees a pearly shine. She scoops up a handful of sand. Keeping her hand underwater, she lets the sand sift away between her fingers until all that's left is a pale pink shell. "Hey, look, Colleen. A flamingo tongue. They're hard to find!"

"Big whoop. Can we go inside now? I'm dying out here!"

They walk back to the Farrells', Colleen complaining about the heat the whole way. When they reach the house, Mrs. Farrell is taking a nap. She's left sandwiches on the table for them. The two girls eat their lunch in silence. Mica doesn't even want to be at the Farrells' anymore, but when Colleen says she's going to read, Mica feels betrayed.

Mica asks George to drive her home. Colleen rides along with a book open in her lap. *Probably wants to make sure I don't laugh at any of her brother's jokes,* Mica thinks.

When they reach Bert's Marina, Mica climbs out. "Thanks, George." She doesn't smile at him, afraid it might look like sucking up.

"Bye, Mica." George drums a rhythm on the truck door with his fingers. "I hate to say this, but Colleen is beginning to rub off on you. You look as grumpy as she does."

Colleen hasn't taken her nose out of the book since they got in the car, so Mica risks a smile and says, "Bye, George." She glances at the top of her friend's head; Colleen's engrossed in the book. She's not listening. "Bye, Leeny!"

Colleen's eyes snap right up out of the book. She stares at Mica without blinking. Mica had been so sure Colleen wouldn't hear that she took a chance on the hated nickname, just to be in on George's joke. "Sorry! I was kidding."

Without ever saying a word, Colleen erases Mica by returning to her book. Mica knows Colleen wants her to think that wherever she is in her alternate world, it's more real and important than working things out with her here-and-now best friend. But Colleen's face is red, and unless she can fake them too, those are real tears in her eyes.

Mica feels terrible. She wasn't trying to hurt Colleen's feelings. But she *was* sucking up to George, her borrowed brother. She knew she shouldn't and she did it anyway.

Dear Anna,

This is a flamingo tongue shell (<u>Cyphoma gibbosum</u>).
Colleen and I found it in the park behind the library.
Correction: I found it. To find it, Colleen would have had
to go in the water, and she doesn't do saltwater.

Colleen is my friend, but she's way different from me.
There are things about me she could never understand.
I think you could, because our lives have been sort of the
same. You asked about my mother, and I never told you,
but as my friend it's okay for you to know. My mom
walked out on us. All I have is her wedding ring—guess
she didn't need it anymore. The Captain got rid of the
rest of her stuff. He said we had to travel light if we
were going to live aboard the <u>Martina.</u> We've been
traveling light ever since.

I still miss her, but it's getting hard to remember her.
Sometimes Aunt Emma acts like a mom, but a real mom
would love me and the Captain both. Aunt Emma doesn't
love the Captain, that's for sure! I don't think she even
approves of him. Sometimes he drinks too much. He's still
a good dad but I worry about him.

I wish you weren't so far away. I wish we could talk.

Your SS,
Mica

chapter 22

Wednesday, April 30

THE DONATION JAR TO HELP injured birds has been sitting on the counter at Bert's Marina for months. To Emma, collecting for the Wild Bird Rescue Center seems only fair. A lot of the bird injuries come from hooks and fishing lines, the very things she sells every day. Sometimes a little loose change plinks into the jar, but most of the time it just sits there keeping one little circle on the counter from getting dusty.

She's looked at that jar off and on all day, not because of the injured birds, but because of the envelope propped against it. It's the letter from Anna Casey she picked up this morning with the marina mail. "Something's wrong," she tells Bert when he comes inside to get himself a can of soda. "There's nothing in this envelope but a letter."

His ginger ale fizzes as he pulls the tab. "Maybe she ran out of stuff to send."

"And what about this?" She holds up the envelope. On the back, where Anna usually draws dogs and suns, are the words "No news yet."

"She's a kid," Bert says. "It could mean anything. Open it if you're worried."

"Oh, I can't! It's addressed to Mica!"

"Guess you'll have to wait then." And he ambles back out.

Emma is holding the letter up to the window to see if she can read through the envelope when the Captain wanders in. She saw him leave early this morning to take Mica to school. When he returned he climbed aboard the *Martina*, and as far as she knows he hasn't been topside all day. "Are you sick?" she asks him.

"I need a Coke." He sticks his head in the soda cooler and then just stands there.

Emma hates it when someone holds the door open. It fogs the glass and runs up the electric bill. "You're letting out the cold." But she feels a little sorry for him. As he rummages for a Coke at the back of the case, she can't help noticing how skinny his legs have become.

He finally chooses a can and slides the door shut. He pops the top and pours soda down his throat. There are dark circles under his eyes and his cheeks seem hollowed out—and no one should drink soda that fast. As he sets the empty can down on the counter, Emma wonders if she smells alcohol.

"I'll pick up Mica if you want," she says. "I could use a thing or two from Winn-Dixie."

"No, no, I'll do it." He pays for the Coke and a roll of breath mints, then aims his body at the door—and misses. His shoulder slams against the door frame. Emma doesn't dare follow him to watch him walk down the dock to the moped; he might think she's spying. But she stands behind the screen door at the front of the office to watch unobserved as he speeds away. "Oh, mercy!" He very nearly falls over when he hits a deep patch of gravel. The truck he doesn't see when he pulls onto the highway honks at him long and loud.

"You see that?" Bert sticks his head inside. "He came darned close to being a hood ornament."

In a moment, Bert is banging on something again. Emma goes back to her stool. *Emma Floyd,* she scolds herself, *I hope you didn't just do a very stupid thing by letting him go.* She spared Dr. Delano's feelings, but if anything happens to him or—God forbid—Mica, she will never forgive herself.

The minutes stretch. She's just convinced herself they're both dead when she hears the buzz of the moped engine. "Thank you!" she says to the gray concrete ceiling.

It isn't long before Mica comes drooping in. She probably wants a ride to Colleen's. A long face is her usual way of starting that conversation.

But instead of talking, Mica sits on her stool, crosses her arms on the counter, and puts her head down.

"Mica? Are you okay?" The girl's shoulder blades lift like stubby wings as she shrugs. "There's a letter from Anna."

"A letter?" She snatches up the envelope, excited, then frowns. "Why is it so flat?" She reads Anna's scrawl on the back of the envelope. "'No news yet'?" She looks up at Emma. "What does *that* mean?"

"Open it and we'll know." Emma sounds cheerful, but finds herself leaning anxiously toward Mica as she tears the letter open. The gnawing sense that something bad has happened has been with her all day.

As Mica smooths the letter on the counter, Emma reads over her shoulder. "Goodness!" she says, covering her heart with her hand.

Dear Mica,

I am so so scared! Cody got hurt today after school and it was all my fault! We were climbing the Old Senator—we wrote you that letter from up there, remember?

Cody's not a bad climber, but he's too little to go high and I let him. In fact I helped him. When he wanted to go just a little higher, I told him that was far enough. I could see the next branch was too weak. Now I'd give anything if I had stopped him. When he grabbed it, the branch broke and he fell out of the tree!

Luckily Mr. Webster and Miss J came home at exactly that second because when Cody hit the ground he wasn't moving. I could tell he was hurt bad. He didn't open his eyes even when Mr. Webster talked to him. It took forever for the ambulance to get there because it got caught on the other side of the railroad track waiting for a train to pass. Cody still wasn't awake when they rushed him to the hospital.

It's four thirty in the morning now—so I guess that the accident really happened yesterday. It all runs together since Miss J and I haven't been to bed yet. She's sitting in her chair. She doesn't know she's asleep. If she did, she'd wake herself up and get back to worrying. I don't think anyone else in the neighborhood is asleep, though. Mr. and Mrs. Floyd are at the hospital along with Mr. Webster. Ben is staying over at Justin's, but I can see the lights on there and at Cass's and Jemmie's.

The sky is getting that milky look. The sun is about to rise. No one has come home from the hospital or called to let us know that Cody is okay. The Floyds probably won't call us since it was my fault he got hurt, but I'm hoping Mr. Webster will.

Cody just has to be all right. But will he? I know about accidents. Everything can be fine one second and over the next. It happened to my parents.

There's probably a special place for foster kids who hurt other kids—a boot camp or a jail. I hope they'll let me write you from there.

Please tell Aunt Emma that I'm sorry. I hope she doesn't hate me for hurting her nephew. If she does I understand.

I have never been so scared in my life.

Your ss,
Anna

p.s. I'm going to put this out for the mailman now. If I hear anything else about Cody, I'll write again.

"Bert!" Aunt Emma's yell makes Mica jump, she was so deep into the letter. "Bert Floyd, get in here right this very minute!"

Mica hears a grunt and a bang, followed by a "Dagnabbit!" which is as close as Uncle Bert gets to cursing.

"Bert!"

"I'm moving as fast as I can, woman! What seems to be the problem? Is the world coming to an end?" Uncle Bert huffs into the shop wearing a large splash of motor oil on the front of his overalls.

Mica runs at him waving the letter. "Cody's hurt! He fell out of a tree and they took him away in an ambulance!"

For just a second the irises of his eyes, usually half-hidden by folds of saggy skin, show all the way around. "Must be some mistake," he says. Before taking the letter from her hand, he pulls a pair of drugstore glasses out of the pocket at the top of his overall bib and settles them on his face. He squints through them, mumbling Anna's words under his breath. When he finishes, he closes his eyes for a second. Mica wonders if he's saying a prayer.

"Now, Emma," he says, opening his eyes again and peering at his wife over the tops of his glasses. "Let's think a minute. Today's Wednesday. Anna wrote this Saturday morning. You know if the boy was in bad shape we would've had a phone call by now."

Mica hugs herself while Uncle Bert dials one of the numbers penciled on the wall. "We'll just clear this all up," he says, hitting the last number. He gazes at the ceiling and whistles nervously between his teeth. "Okay. It's ringing. One ring...two...three."

Mica holds her breath but nothing happens.

"Pick it up, pick it up," Uncle Bert mutters. "Dang it! Answering machine." He lifts his glasses and props them against his shiny forehead, waiting for the beep so he can leave a message. "Mike, Samantha? This is Uncle Bert. Nothing special going on here, but could you give us a call when you get the chance?"

"What?" says Aunt Emma as he hangs up the phone. "Call when you get the chance?"

"I didn't want to scare 'em!"

"How can *you* scare *them*? They know all about it. You're not going to tell them anything new by mentioning that Cody fell out of a tree."

"I taught Cody how to swim," Mica murmurs, too low for the Floyds to hear. "And he was always way nicer to me than his brother was. I can see why Anna likes him." She runs a finger along the edge of the counter. An idea pops into her head. "Hey, you guys! Why don't we call Anna?"

Aunt Emma turns to her husband. "We could, you know, Bert! How many Johnette Walkers could there be in Tallahassee, Florida?"

"I'm surprised there's even one," says Uncle Bert.

Mica knows the address by heart. She recites it. Aunt Emma gets the number from information.

"I'll call!" Mica holds out her hand.

"No, dear. Cody is our nephew."

Mica goes back to hugging herself, and Aunt Emma dials.

Family, according to the Captain, is just "an accident of biology," but people with families don't seem to look at it that way. Aunt Emma is calling Miss Johnette because she's the aunt. But being family doesn't mean you own all the happiness when things go right—or all the sadness when things go wrong. Mica is sure she's just as worried as they are.

She edges closer to Aunt Emma, hoping the person on the other end will be a loud talker.

It seems as if no one will answer the phone there either when Aunt Emma suddenly stands up a little straighter. "Hello?" She says it as if she were the one receiving the call. "This is Emma Floyd? Calling from the Keys?"

Why does she make everything sound like a question? Mica wonders. *She knows who she is.*

"Yes, yes! That's right!" Aunt Emma sounds relieved. The person on the other end of the line must have agreed that she's Emma Floyd from the Keys. "Is this Johnette Walker?"

"Is it?" Mica leans against Aunt Emma, trying to hear both halves of the conversation. She can hear the voice on the other end—the person *is* a loud talker—but she can't make out the words.

"We just got a letter from Anna and our hearts are absolutely in our throats. Did Cody really fall out of the Old Senator?" Aunt Emma nods vigorously. "Uh huh…uh huh."

Mica and Uncle Bert hover around Aunt Emma like moths around a lightbulb. Aunt Emma listens for what seems like forever before covering the receiver with one hand. "He's more or less fine. He came to that morning." She takes her hand off the receiver. "What was that? Oh." She laughs, and the hand covers the receiver again. "She says the first thing he said was 'Boy, am I hungry!'"

Uncle Bert nods. "Sounds like our Cody."

"Then he asked why his head hurt so much."

"Why did it?" Mica asks, bouncing on her toes.

"I'm finding that out now! Uh huh…uh huh…"

Uncle Bert sputters, "Speak English, woman!"

But all Aunt Emma says is, "Yes, yes, I understand."

"Thank heavens one of us does," Uncle Bert mutters, stowing his hands behind the bib of his overalls and rocking back on his heels.

"Is that your doorbell?" Aunt Emma asks. "It's all right, Johnette. You better run…. Mica? Yes, she's right here. Sure, I'll put her on. Mica, Anna wants to speak to you."

The phone is warm from being held, and maybe from all the worry that has gone both ways down the line. "Hello?" says Mica, suddenly shy.

At first there's no answer, and then the words rush at her. "Mica. It's me, Anna. Everything is terrible!"

"I know," Mica says. She almost adds that things are terrible for her too, but things are worse for her friend. "Cody's going to be all right, isn't he?"

"Yes…but…" Anna hesitates. Her voice is lower than Mica thought it would be. Low, but nice. "Oh, Mica. I broke his arm!"

"No, you didn't! Not personally."

"But it's broken because of me." Anna nearly whispers the next words. Mica can barely hear. "I'm so scared. What if they take me away from Miss J?"

"No way! Why would they do that?"

"*I* made him fall, but *she* built the ladder, and she wasn't home when Cody climbed the tree. But even if she had been home she would've let him climb. She lets kids climb trees. She encourages them. She's not like a regular mother."

"She sounds better."

"Way better, but Mrs. Riley and the other Social Services people mostly care about a kid's safety. Oh, Mica. I could never be happy with anyone but Miss J."

"Do you have to tell Mrs. Riley?

"Miss J says we do. And then what will happen?"

Mica finds herself staring at the letter on the counter—and she gets the strangest feeling. It's as if her heart is a flower bud that has suddenly decided to open in the middle of her chest.

What if she could fix everything? "I have an idea," she says to Anna. "What if I write a letter to Mrs. Riley? A letter of support?" Letters of support have helped manatees, whales, and all kinds of endangered animals. Why not Anna? "The Captain will sign it too; they've probably heard of him. And Aunt Emma will sign. I'll send it to you and you can give it to her."

"But you don't even know Miss J."

"I know about her from you. I'm sure a letter will help." Mica hears a man's voice in the background.

"I better go," says Anna. "Please write the letter soon. Don't forget."

"I will. Promise." Mica fingers the dolphin charm on the chain around her neck. As she hangs up she decides that she'll put the good luck charm in the letter to Mrs. Riley. It may not be scientific, but if there is such a thing as luck Anna needs it now.

chapter 23

ANNA WALKS SLOWLY TOWARD the Floyds' house, clutching a bunch of spiderwort flowers. It's a pretty weird bouquet. Spiderwort flowers are tiny and they wither in the afternoon—too bad it's afternoon. But the summer flowers aren't blooming yet and the spring azaleas and dogwoods are way past flowering. She saw pale pink evening primroses growing along the cemetery fence, but Aunt Eva had warned her, "Always hold your breath when you walk by a cemetery." She said anything connected with a cemetery is bad luck. Anna didn't know if her aunt was right, but her luck had been so bad lately that she held her breath, walked fast, and avoided the pretty flowers nodding against the fence.

After gathering the scrawny spiderworts at the edge of the road, she stopped at home, let Beauty out, and wrote Miss J a note. While Beauty sniffed around the yard Anna splashed cool water on the spiderworts. It didn't help.

Now she's walking up the path to Cody's door. The flowers are drippy and droopy, but they're something to hide behind. What if he doesn't want to see her?

He was released from the hospital Sunday morning. Cass says he's fine, but maybe she's just being nice. He hasn't gone back to school yet.

Anna stands at the Floyds' front door trying to get up enough nerve to knock. The bouquet shakes. She knocks so softly she can hardly hear it herself. She knocks again, this time like she means it.

The door opens partway and Mrs. Floyd looks out. Anna can see a little of the long flowered skirt she wears. "Hi, Anna," she says quietly.

"Mrs. Floyd, I'm so sorry."

"I know you are, Anna. And he's fine. But he won't be climbing trees anytime soon."

"Can I please see him?"

"Not now, honey, he's resting. But I can give him those flowers."

"Is he mad at me?"

"Cody?" Mrs. Floyd smiles. "Cody doesn't get mad at anyone, but he's sleeping right now. He's had lots of company in the last hour. His brother brought everyone home from school with him. I had to shoo them away. They all went over to Jemmie's for a snack."

"Mom? Is someone there?" The voice that calls from the back of the house is as skinny as a stray cat.

"Cody!" Anna calls. "Cody, you sound terrible!"

Mrs. Floyd puts a hand on Anna's shoulder and whispers, "He's just trying to get sympathy. He felt left out when everyone took off for ice cream at the Lewises' house." In a louder voice she calls out, "Anna's here, Cody. Do you feel well enough to see another visitor?"

"I guess…" Cody's voice is even thinner, as thin as a thread that's about to break.

Anna walks into his room, the bouquet in front of her face.

"Flowers?" Cody sputters, forgetting to sound pathetic. "Flowers? I'm not a girl!"

Anna lowers the bouquet. "No, but you're supposed to get flowers when you're hurt. You know, for a boy who fell out of a tree you look pretty good."

Cody sags back against his pillows. "Hey, want to sign my cast? I saved you the best spot." He points to the back of his elbow. "Sign it 'Arm-Breaker Anna,' okay?"

Anna's stomach lurches. She can't write that! It's incriminating. It could make things worse with Social Services. Instead she writes, "Your Friend, Anna." Cody can't see the back of his elbow anyway.

"Hey," says Cody. "Wanna see the zipper?"

"What zipper?"

"The head zipper." His chin drops to his chest. What little hair he had on the back of his head has been shaved off and the white skin pulled together and stitched as tight as a baseball.

"I didn't know you cut your head *that* bad!"

"It took twelve stitches. You can count 'em if you want."

But Anna collapses on the edge of the bed. "Does it hurt?" she asks.

"Like crazy," he groans.

She can feel her lips quiver.

"Well, it's not really that bad," he admits. "But it's hard to lie down on. And my ribs hurt when I take a deep breath." He breathes and winces, breathes and winces. "Want to see my bruises?"

At least I won't have to spend my whole life feeling bad for him, Anna thinks as she walks home. *He'll be okay.*

It's something, but not much. Soon she may be packing all the rocks in her collection, the clothes from her cousins, the maps she's made of all the neighborhoods she's lived in. She'll beg them to let her take Beauty, but they probably won't—she's never heard of a foster dog. And what will she do without Miss J? Her arms and legs feel so heavy she can barely walk. She's watching the toes of her Ben Franklin shoes when she hears the kids' voices.

She rounds the corner and there they are, sitting on the stone wall in front of Miss J's. It's not as if they're waiting for her. They've settled there like birds on a telephone wire.

"Hey, Anna," Ben calls. "You look like your dog died."

"I just visited your brother."

"Why so sad? You didn't kill him." He twirls a basketball on his finger. "You didn't even break him bad. Just one little bone in his arm. I bet when he goes back to school they'll have a party for him."

"And he likes the scar," says Cass, scooching closer to Ben so Anna can sit down.

"Right," says Jemmie. "The zipper!"

"It's like his new pet," Justin adds.

"Yeah, falling out of that tree was one of the best things that ever happened to him." Ben tosses the ball up and catches it. "I tell you, Anna, he's getting a charge out of it."

Anna pulls her hands deep inside the sleeves of her cousin's sweater, folding the ends up inside her clenched fists. Before last week she would have given anything to be sitting here with Ben, Cass, Jemmie, and Justin. If they're nice to her now, it's just one more thing she'll lose when she gets taken away from Miss J.

"Heads up, Anna!" Ben says. He holds the ball in his finger-tips, ready to pass it to her over Cass's head, but Anna's hands stay hidden in her sleeves. "Come on, catch it!" He jumps off the wall and falls back a couple of steps, ready to throw it, but when her arms stay at her sides he shrugs and begins tossing the ball from hand to hand.

Jemmie jumps down, too, clapping her hands. "Come on, Ben, give it here." She catches it, but when she looks at Anna she rests the ball against one hip. "He's fine, Anna. Get over it!"

"He'll be fine eventually," Anna concedes. "But when Social Services hears about it, they'll probably take me away from Miss J."

"No way!" Jemmie taps the toe of her sneaker on the pavement. "He climbed a tree and he fell out. Is that *your* fault? I don't *think* so."

Anna wishes she was like Jemmie. Jemmie is so sure about everything. "But I made him climb higher than he should have. And Miss J built the ladder. She lets kids climb. What if Mrs. Riley decides she's irresponsible?"

"Parents do irresponsible things all the time." Justin rubs a drip of ice cream into the leg of his jeans. "Mine, for instance. If you want, I'll make a list. You can show it to Mrs. Riley."

"But they're your real parents. They're allowed to make mistakes. I'm not Miss J's kid yet. Until they give me over, I belong to the state of Florida."

Justin licks a finger and rubs the stain again. "Like those convicts by the side of the road with the striped shirts."

"Hey!" scolds Jemmie. "You mind keeping stuff like that to yourself?"

"I talked to Mica the other night." Anna bounces the rubber heels of her shoes against the wall. "She's going to write a letter of support. Do you think it could help? She's never even met Miss J."

Ben flips the ball slowly from hand to hand. "What if my folks write a letter?" he says. "They don't blame Miss J. They like her."

He stops and hugs the ball to his chest. "Hey, Cody can write one too! He's the injured party. He can't write with that arm, but he could dictate. Who should we write the letters to?"

"I guess Mrs. Riley. But tell Cody he can't mention all the soda he drinks at Miss J's."

"Don't worry." Ben grins. "I'll be the guy with the pen. Consider it not mentioned."

"I better get home and set the table," Cass says, but before sliding down off the wall she gives Anna a quick hug. "Everything will be okay."

As they walk away, the others pass the ball back and forth. When they reach the corner they go their separate ways. "Don't forget," Anna calls after Ben.

Cass walks backward for a few steps. "Don't worry. I'll make sure he does it tonight."

Anna knows that all the letters in the world may not help— but at least it's worth a try.

It's time for her to go inside too, but she sits by herself on the wall. The VW is in the driveway. Since she went to Cody's with the bouquet, Miss J has come home from the high school. Anna's checked on Cody, now it's time to check on Miss J. Her foster mom hasn't been the same since the night Cody fell. Whether she's lesson planning, cooking, or grading papers, her mind seems to be somewhere else. She never whistles. Anna wonders if they'll ever do the chicken dance of joy again.

Anna's about to go inside when a muddy pickup rattles into their driveway. "Mr. Webster!" She jumps down off the wall.

As the driver's door opens, Trog runs across Mr. Webster's lap and explodes into the street. The dog runs at Anna, jumps up on her, then uses her as a springboard. He turns ninety degrees in the air and dashes up to the house, barking for Beauty.

Mr. Webster's work boots are the next thing out of the truck. They're old and worn and one of the laces is knotted where it broke. The boots are sturdy and dependable, just like their owner.

"Hi, Anna," he says, walking over to her.

"Hi, Mr. Webster." He doesn't complain about being called Mr. Webster any more. The last thing he said about it was the day after Cody got hurt: "We'll come up with something better when things settle down."

She clings to the comment because it's like a promise that things *will* settle down and that when they do, she'll still be here to call him something. But he must be worried too. He insisted that Miss J wait until they knew Cody was going to be okay before calling Social Services. Anna doesn't know whether or not she's made the call yet. She's afraid to ask.

He jingles the change in his pocket. "Care to guess?" This is a game he invented after the accident, hoping to distract her.

She pushes at the inside of her cheek with her tongue and listens carefully. "Two nickels and a penny?"

"Not even close!" He fishes in his pocket. "One quarter, two dimes, a Canadian penny, and a fossilized shark tooth." He holds it all out on his palm.

"A Canadian penny is cheating!"

"How about the shark tooth?"

"I could probably guess that."

He laughs. "Maybe so. I'm a shark-tooth kind of guy."

She watches him drop the coins and the shark tooth back in his pocket. "I went to see Cody," she says softly.

"Oh?" He studies her with serious eyes. "How is he?"

"Okay I guess." She doesn't stiffen when he puts an arm around her shoulders. She wonders if Miss J ever noticed that he smells like leaves. "He's got a big scar on the back of his head."

"Bigger than this?" Mr. Webster stops to show her the scar that zags across the top of his forehead and disappears into his hair.

"I think it's a tie," she says, although Cody's is bigger. "How did you get yours?"

"My brother beaned me with his lunch box. You'll meet him one of these days. Maybe you can help me get even with him."

Mr. Webster pays attention to her now and Anna likes it. She knows Miss J talked to him about Aunt Emma's letter and the conversation she and Miss J had about him. "Thanks for letting me live," he'd said. And then he'd pulled an imaginary noose tight around his neck, crossed his eyes, and let his tongue hang out.

Now they go up the walk together. By the time they get to the purple door, Trog has put a few eager scratches in the paint. Anna hears Beauty working on the other side. "No puppy treats for you guys," Mr. Webster tells the dogs, but before grabbing Trog's collar he gives Anna's shoulder a squeeze.

chapter 24

MRS. RILEY CARRIES THE CASE FILE to her car, amazed at how thick it is all of a sudden. She had barely heard of the incident—Johnette Walker waited to call until the boy was out of danger—when the letters began pouring in.

The first envelope contained letters from three different writers: Anna's pen pal in the Keys, the pen pal's father, and a woman who said she was the injured boy's aunt—although what she was also doing in the Keys was a mystery to Mrs. Riley.

The envelope was addressed to "Mrs. Riley c/o Anna Casey." Someone, probably Anna, had crossed out Anna's address and written the address of the agency on it. She's sure Anna never opened it. If she had, she would have found the small silver charm her pen pal included along with the scrap of paper that said, "Ben, Cody, and I found this silver dolphin. I *know* it's good luck!"

She opens the folder. The girl's letter is on top.

To: Mrs. Riley c/o Anna Casey
Dear Mrs. Riley:

You may not know this, but kids are born to climb trees and jump off the masts of sailboats and swim in deep water. A few break bones or get eaten by sharks but if they don't get hurt or get eaten, they grow up better. Not all moms understand that, but Miss J does. You should give her a medal, not take Anna away from her.

It's hard to find a good mother if you lose your real one. Don't make Anna start over!

Sincerely,
Anna's Sorta Sister,
Mica Delano

Dear Ms. Riley:

This is Mica's father, Dr. Robin Michael Delano. I want to reiterate what my daughter wrote and add that young animals with mothers fare better biologically than those without. Although Johnette Walker and Anna Casey are not genetically related, they have formed a parent-child bond that should not be broken.

In addition, Anna is fortunate to have a foster mother who is scientifically aware. She will give the girl a strong academic start. The accident was unfortunate. There may even have been some carelessness, but everyone makes mistakes.

Best regards,
Dr. Robin Michael Delano

Dear Mrs. Riley!

I'm Cody's aunt, Emma Floyd, and that boy can be a bit of a scamp. I'm sure that climbing that tree was as much his idea as anyone's. I have been enjoying Anna's letters for months and feel as if I know her and her foster mother. They seem so happy together. Remember, where there is love there is family. Please do not tear this family apart!

Sincerely,

Emma Floyd

Mrs. Riley shakes her head. What letters! Her favorite part is the line about kids being born to fall out of trees. Although she could never say it at work, Mrs. Riley is inclined to agree. Most kids spend too much time watching TV or playing video games. A few healthy accidents are part of raising a strong, independent child.

But she can't understand why the pen pal, and even the adults, thought she would take Anna away from Johnette Walker. Where did *that* idea come from? Don't these people know she's in the business of strengthening families, not tearing them apart?

And the letters from the Keys were just the first batch. Under that one are letters from neighbors and one from the family of the boy who broke his arm—all supporting Miss J. But her favorite came from the boy himself, the one who fell out of the tree. The original is in her folder, but a photocopy hangs on the bulletin board over her desk.

Dear Mrs. Riley,

Please don't make Anna go away. She is my Friend. Miss J is her real mom even If she isn't because they picked each other and now no one can unpick them.

My arm doesn't even hurt anymore and the scar on my head Looks Like a zipper so I Like it. If you give Anna to someone Else I'll go over and Fall out of their tree too so why bother?

Please. Please. Please Leave Anna with Miss J. They would miss each other very bad.

Your Friend,
Cody Floyd

(written down by Ben Floyd)

As she places the file in the empty passenger seat, Mrs. Riley admits that she can't pretend that the incident wasn't serious. It will definitely cause a world of paperwork. It already has. She backs the car into the street thinking, *If there is one thing I hate, it's paperwork.*

Then she remembers Anna the day she drove her to her first foster home. Her floppy denim hat was pulled way down. The eyes beneath the brim were so scared and so hopeful. The boy who rode with her that day, Eb Gramlich, is back with his truly irresponsible mother and, like so many of the children she's worked with, is as lost as a leaf in the wind.

But not Anna.

Anna is that rare child who has been found.

Mrs. Riley smiles as she drives toward the cottage with the purple door. The lucky dolphin charm is in her wallet. She looks forward to putting it in Anna's hand. This is the part of her job that she likes—reassuring good people that everything is going to be all right. In the end, she has to agree with Cody Floyd. Anna Casey and Johnette Walker picked each other, and no one—not even the state of Florida—can unpick them.

chapter 25

THE CAPTAIN HAS BARELY TOUCHED the bowl of Dinty Moore beef stew Mica put in front of him. She keeps begging him to eat, but all he does is rearrange the vegetables with his fork. He does this all the time now and it scares her. She wishes she were somewhere else.

"Finals are coming up," she says. "I'll probably go to Colleen's tomorrow to study and maybe spend the night." She hasn't been invited, but she plans to call her from the marina office first thing in the morning. If she mentions finals, Colleen will just *have* to ask her over.

"Busy, busy." The Captain pushes a carrot to the other side of the bowl. "You're always busy now that you have a friend."

But if he thinks that, he hasn't been paying attention. He hasn't noticed that Colleen hardly ever invites her over anymore, that most nights she's alone on the boat.

Mica misses the blue house and the shell-lined garden. She misses Mrs. Farrell and her number one brother, George. At Colleen's she can forget that she's worried about her father and pretend she's part of Colleen's family.

He sets down his fork. "Exceptional dinner," he announces. "But I couldn't eat another bite!" Smiling brightly, he pushes the bowl away.

She can tell he's about to get to his feet and say something about meeting someone across the creek. Strictly business, of course. But even if he doesn't notice things, she does. Always on the thin side, her father is turning bone-skinny. "Four bites," she says.

"What?"

"You can't go anywhere until you eat four bites."

He sags back in the seat. "Who's the parent around here?"

"Four bites," she repeats, picking up his fork and handing it back to him.

He stabs a tiny piece of beef.

"Four *real* bites."

"All right, all right!" The beef chunk slides up the fork as he jabs a potato. "Happy?" he asks and shoves it in his mouth.

By the time she's gotten him to swallow four real bites, she's exhausted—too exhausted to put up a fight when he makes his announcement about business across the creek and leaves her alone on the boat.

She can't go to bed yet. It's too early. But she feels so defeated that she pushes her own bowl and the pot of stew aside and puts her head down on her arms.

She wants, worse than anything, to be safe at Colleen's house. She thinks about what she could say to her friend that would guarantee an invitation. *Hey, Colleen, I took great notes. Hey, Colleen, I'll help you with science.*

They still hang out together at school, but sometimes Mica thinks it's because they're stuck with each other, like two people on a desert island. Except for being smart and good at school, all they have in common is the fact that no one else pays attention to them. The last few times Mica has asked to come over, Colleen has said she was busy. Rules or no rules, Colleen doesn't to want to share her family.

Now, even though it's only in her imagination, Mica returns to the Farrells' kitchen. She and Mrs. Farrell are having a friendly conversation when she drifts off to sleep.

She doesn't wake up until one in the morning, her neck stiff from sleeping with her head on the table. The stew looks greasy-cold. She can tell just by the way the *Martina* tugs sadly at its ropes that she's alone. But to make sure, she checks her father's cabin. His sheets and blanket have been kicked to the foot of the bunk. The unmade berth sends a shiver through her. The Captain used to be so tidy.

Mica climbs up into her own bunk. All the faces of all the friends who have gone away grin from the walls of her cabin. She realizes that she doesn't have one picture of Colleen. All she has is a recipe for cinnamon buns she can't even make.

Without taking her clothes off, she crawls into her sleeping bag.

What wakes her at six is the silence. No one snores as loudly as the Captain, but all Mica hears as she stares at the white vinyl ceiling above her berth is the creak of a fender as the incoming tide pins the *Martina* against the dock. The feeling that shoots through her is cold and electric.

Where is he? He always comes home, no matter what.

She kicks the sleeping bag off and races to the deck and turns into the wind. Her hair, just beginning to grow back, blows around her face. She has to hold it back with one hand to see. No one is there except a pelican on a piling. The outdoor bar across the creek closed a long time ago. The stools are deserted. Still, the only thing she can think to do is walk across the bridge and look for him.

She drops from the sailboat to the dock. Her flip-flops wait right where she left them, their toes curled up from spending so much time in the sun. She's wiggling her left foot under the rubber strap when she sees the front wheel of the moped sticking out of the grass at the edge of the parking lot. "Captain!" she screams. She runs straight for him, gravel biting her bare heel, the single flip-flop snapping against the other foot.

She's still a few feet away when she hears the world-famous marine biologist's world-famous snore. She circles him once, then drops to her knees. A long gouge in the gravel ends at his back tire. He must have barreled into the lot, skidded, and laid the bike down in the grass. His chin and one arm are scraped, but he's sleeping peacefully, one leg under the bike.

How will she get him back to the boat? She's trying to wake him when someone shouts, "Mica!" Aunt Emma in a flowered nightgown and Uncle Bert in his underwear bustle up the short embankment to the parking lot, panting hard. With Uncle Bert's hairy knees on one side and Aunt Emma's bird-like bony legs on the other, Mica feels surrounded.

"Bert!" Aunt Emma gasps. "Call an ambulance!"

Mica grabs the hem of Aunt Emma's nightgown. "No, he's fine. Really, he's okay. He's just sleeping."

"Heck of a place to sleep!" Uncle Bert roars.

"It's all right. I'll get him inside." Mica jumps to her feet. "He had a little accident, but he's fine." She prods the Captain with her bare foot, trying to wake him up before the Floyds do something drastic.

The Captain lets out an embarrassing snort. "What the...?" He blinks up at the bright sky, then squeezes his eyes shut. "Where am I?"

Uncle Bert crosses his arms on top of his belly. "You're flat on your can in the weeds."

The Captain squints at him with one bloodshot eye. "Bert? You're in your underwear."

"I'm out here in my skivvies because some drunk took a header in my parking lot."

"He's not a drunk!" Mica shouts.

"Emma," says Uncle Bert. "Get Mica to the houseboat. Give her something to eat." He stares down at the man on the ground. "This mess has gone on long enough. You want to throw your own life away, fine. But you're endangering your daughter and I can't allow that."

Mica steps between Uncle Bert and the Captain. "Leave us alone, please. We can take care of ourselves!"

"Come away now, honey." Aunt Emma sing-songs the words as if she were talking to a little kid. "Let Uncle Bert clean him up. He's got gravel in his face."

The Captain pushes himself up to a sitting position. "I'm...fine," he gasps.

That's when Mica gets a good look at the nasty scrape on his chin. Aunt Emma is right about the gravel. If Uncle Bert doesn't do it, she'll have to pick it out of the cut with tweezers. The thought makes the backs of her knees feel weak, but she knows she can do it. "Go back to bed now," she says. "Please go back to bed."

Aunt Emma's arm encircles Mica's shoulders. The arm, which looks like little more than loose old skin draped over bone, is surprisingly strong. "Uncle Bert was a medic in the army." She turns Mica away from the Captain. "He'll take good care of your dad."

"But he's okay!" Mica tries to shrug off Aunt Emma's protective arm. "This is nothing! We got caught in a tropical storm once. We lost our mast, but we survived. I can take care of him!"

"It's best to let Uncle Bert handle this." Aunt Emma's voice is soothing but firm.

As they walk away, Mica hears Uncle Bert say, "Think you can get to your feet?"

When the Captain doesn't answer, she looks back. Her father is kneeling in the gravel, staring at his own hands.

"No!" Mica protests. "I'm not going!"

Aunt Emma hesitates with her hand on the phone. "But you *always* want to go to Colleen's. I'll just give the Farrells a quick call."

"I said no. The Captain needs me!"

"You poor girl!" Abandoning the phone, Aunt Emma wraps her arms around Mica. "You've taken responsibility for your father for years," she croons. "It's time for adults to take over."

Although the voice is sweet, Mica is scared breathless. She pushes Emma Floyd away. "I want to talk to my father!" She runs out the door. Ducking a basket of fake flowers, she leaps to the dock and sprints the short distance between the boats. "Captain!" She bounds onto the deck of the *Martina* and down the companionway ladder. She finds Uncle Bert in the galley washing last night's dishes. "You don't need to do that. I always do the dishes. I just fell asleep!"

Uncle Bert flips the dish towel off his shoulder and dries the pot. "Did Emma feed you good?"

"Yes, sir, but—"

"And now you're going to Colleen's, right?"

"No. I mean no, sir."

"I'm afraid you have to, honey. Go on and change your clothes.

I'll meet you at the van in, say, fifteen minutes?" He lumbers toward the ladder, the sailboat rocking gently under his weight.

"I want to stay with my dad. Please?"

Uncle Bert stops. He shakes his head. "All right. For a little while. Come up to the shop when you're ready."

As soon as he leaves, she rushes into her father's cabin. He lies on his bunk. His chin is covered with gauze and tape. Uncle Bert did a more thorough job than she would have. "Captain?" She can't tell if he's asleep. One arm is thrown over his eyes. "Captain?" she says, louder this time. She kneels beside his berth. "Are you all right?"

He moves his arm as if it were very heavy. When it rests on his chest, Mica sees that his eyes are open, but he's not looking at her. "I owe you an apology," he says, staring at the ceiling.

"No, you don't!"

"I do. I couldn't work with Winn. I walked off the grant a week ago."

"Walked off? Why didn't you tell me?"

"I was mad…and ashamed."

"It's okay. Who cares about Winn and his stupid grant anyway? He has sloppy lab technique. You said so yourself."

"That's beside the point. And if I hadn't walked off, he would've asked me to leave. He thinks I've been drinking. And he's right. That grant was so important, but no matter what I did I couldn't work with him. I got scared and frustrated. Before I knew it, I was drinking again. But the grant…Winn…none of that really matters." He finally looks at her. "Uncle Bert says I'm not fit to take care of you." His voice is calm and rational; he's a scientist. But she can see tears in his eyes.

"Who cares about him? *You're* my father! They can't tell you what to do about me!"

"Maybe not, but they can report me for neglect, and if the state finds me unfit they can take you away from me."

"No, they won't! We won't let them," she whispers. "Because we won't be here. We'll cast off and sail away. They won't even know until it's too late. Good-bye, Dr. Winn! Good-bye, school! It'll be just us again." She tugs at his arm, trying to get him to sit up, but he's dead weight.

"It's no use, Mica."

"What are you talking about?" She struggles to drag his legs over to the side of the bunk. He has to get up; they have to go. If they take her away from him she'll be just like Anna. "Hurry! Uncle Bert could come back any minute! The tide's going out. It's perfect."

"Stop it, Mica. Stop!" The Captain sits up on his own, propping his hands against his knees. "Mica, the man is right. I *am* unfit." He hangs his head. "I don't know what to do—I can't lose you—but I can't take care of you either. I have to pull myself together."

"Aunt Emma can watch me and I can watch you."

"She's going away to visit her grandchildren."

The answer immediately pops into her head: Colleen's family. How many times has she imagined moving into her friend's house? And now would be perfect. Colleen will be gone soon. Mica would have Mrs. Farrell and George all to herself.

But she doesn't say a thing. In the stillness she hears the small waves slapping the hull and the quiet tick of the fittings against the mast. The *Martina* is her home. The Captain is her family. This is where she belongs.

She rises up on her knees so she can look into his eyes. "*I'm* fit, Captain. When you get better you can take care of me again. Until then I'll take care of you."

Her father puts his arms around her neck. "Oh, Mica. How did I ever let things get this bad?" He leans against her. She has to tighten all her muscles to support his weight, but she can do it. She's strong.

Dear Ms. Walker,

You don't know me personally, but I feel as if
we've met through our daughters' letters. Mica
has painted me as a "famous" biologist, which
makes this a very hard letter to write. Please
know that I would not be writing it if I felt
I had any choice.

I guess the first step to recovery is admitting
I have a problem, so I must tell you that I am
an alcoholic. Most of the time I keep things
under control, but lately that hasn't been the
case.

I probably wouldn't be doing anything even now
except that Bert and Emma Floyd have threatened
to have the state take my daughter away from me
if I don't overcome my problem. I will do
anything to keep from losing my daughter and
yet they are right. I can't take care of her
now. If I am to do the right thing for my
daughter—and yes, for myself too—I have to make
a fresh start, which puts me in the awkward
position of needing to check myself into a
rehabilitation program for about a month.
Normally I would leave Mica with the Floyds,

but Emma is leaving to spend a month with her
grandchildren as she does every summer.
Mica tells me that Anna has mentioned the
possibility of a visit to Tallahassee this
summer. I know that I have no right to make
this request and I know that you have had
troubles of your own (I hope the letters we
sent to Social Services helped), but if you
could take Mica for that month I would be very
grateful. It would ease my mind to have Mica
safely away from here while I do what I must
do. Knowing that she is with a rational fellow
scientist would ease my mind. If you can't do
it, please just say so. My deepest thanks in
advance for considering this request. Whatever
the outcome, I hope that our daughters will
continue their friendship.

Gratefully,
Dr. Robin Michael Delano

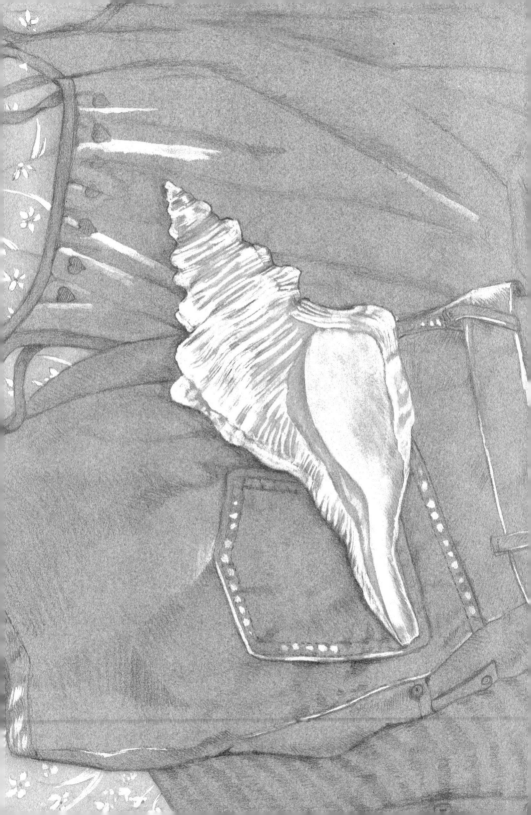

chapter 26

ANNA HOLDS OUT THE SIDES of her short denim skirt—another Goodwill special, but this one still had the original price tag on it. She sees herself reflected in the glass partition that separates the passenger screening area from the rest of the airport. "Do I look okay?"

"You sure I'm the right one to ask?" Miss J wears her usual khaki shorts, purple socks, and Birkenstocks (the warm-weather replacement for her army boots). She hugs a Welcome, Mica! sign in her arms. "Try doing a twirl."

A little nervous, Anna turns in place while Miss J gives her the once-over.

"Just as I suspected. You look perfect!'
Anna grins. "You too."

"Ex*cuse* me," says a businessman dragging a black suitcase on wheels.

"No, excuse us." Miss J and Anna step back and lean against the wall so he can get by. Miss J checks her watch for the fourteenth time. "Only ten more minutes."

"If her flight is on time."

They check the arrival board again. It's been saying "On Time" since they arrived half an hour ago. Now it's flashing "On the Ground…On the Ground…"

"They've landed!" whoops Miss J.

Anna's heart constricts. "Oh my gosh, she's here!"

They crowd as close to the terminal exit as the Homeland Security sign permits. Anna takes off her uncle's old denim hat, then remembers that the latest "adjustment" Miss J made to her haircut wasn't exactly an improvement. She puts the hat back on. Passengers begin to trickle past.

"Excuse me. You fly in from Miami?" Miss J asks a passing woman.

"Uh-huh."

"This is it!" Miss J whispers, squeezing Anna's shoulders.

Mica unbuckles her safety belt. "I can walk out by myself!"

"Just sit tight, dear. You're a UM. When all the other passengers have deplaned I'll walk you up."

Everyone else is grabbing their carry-ons and filing up the aisle. Because of the totally unnecessary "Unaccompanied Minor" tag around her neck, the flight attendant is holding her hostage.

Mica is anxious to meet Anna and Miss J, but more than anything she wants to get to their house so she can call the Captain. Uncle Bert dropped Mica and Aunt Emma at the airport before driving the Captain to the rehab facility. Mica wanted to do it the other way around so she could make sure the place was okay. But the Captain didn't seem to want her to see him check into a program for alcoholics.

When they pulled up to the terminal a speaker was blasting, "The curbside area is for loading and unloading only. Unattended vehicles..." Mica threw her arms around her father and kissed the side of his neck. He didn't kiss her, but he reached into the stuffed backpack between his feet and retrieved a book, a guide to the wildlife of Florida's Big Bend and panhandle. "Consider this a field trip." He choked the words out. "And don't worry about me, okay?"

"Of course not. You'll be fine." But she'll worry about him. She always does.

She could look at the book now while she waits to be set free. Instead, she watches the deplaning passengers: a woman cradling a baby, a couple with four little boys, family members traveling together.

Aunt Emma got her through security and made sure Delta knew she was flying solo. After that she was on her own.

She hopes Anna and Miss J live close to the airport. She can't wait to hear her father's voice.

The flight attendant puts her hands on her knees and leans down. "Ready?" she asks as if speaking to a two-year-old.

"I've been ready."

"You have a carry-on?"

"Uh-huh." Mica hops up on the seat and drags her suitcase out of the overhead bin. She didn't check anything. The clothes Aunt Emma thought were "fit to be seen"—the best of her school clothes—only half-filled the one small suitcase the Captain takes when he goes to conferences. Wrapped in her shorts and T-shirts are biology presents. For Miss J there's a Florida horse conch, *Pleuroploca gigantia*. Before she left, the Captain reminded her, "Tell Miss J that the horse conch is the largest gastropod on the Atlantic coast." He also insisted that she point out that at 18 inches the specimen in her suitcase is near the top size for the species. "Miss J will want to know," he added.

Her present for Anna is a much smaller shell, a channeled

whelk, *Busycon canaliculatum,* but she also brought a channeled whelk egg case. The egg capsules look as if they've been strung together like a necklace; each one is like a small oval change purse. She found it at the washed-up edge of the tide and dried it on the deck of the *Martina.* She'll get Anna to shake it so the tiny whelks inside rattle.

As she drags the suitcase down the aisle of the plane, then through the accordion Jetway, she pretends she's going through the gut of a tube worm. It keeps her mind off being nervous.

The flight attendant's high heels click against the terrazzo floor. Mica struggles to keep the old suitcase upright as the wheels skitter and slide. They pass several "B" gates, the restrooms, and a newsstand.

What if they didn't come? Mica wonders. *What if they forgot? Does Delta Air Lines have a special room where they store unclaimed UMs?*

"Now, who are we looking for?" the flight attendant asks, consulting the paper in her hand. Mica doesn't want to say that she doesn't actually know, except that they're looking for a girl with a haircut that is (hopefully) as bad as hers and a woman who is (almost) as big as a bear.

"Here, hold up the sign. She'll be out any second," Johnette assures Anna. But as she says it she thinks, *Don't let anything go wrong, please.* The line of people coming through has slowed to a dribble.

"You think she's coming? Maybe she missed her flight."

"Aunt Emma would have called us." The usually optimistic Anna looks anxious, and once again Johnette realizes how scared

Anna's been and how long she's had to feel that way. Every bit of her life that she can remember has been uncertain—today can't follow the same sad pattern.

But the minutes pass and the dribble is down to a very slow drip. Anna holds the sign in one hand. The hand hangs at her side. It doesn't reassure Johnette when the pilot and a crew member saunter past, their little wing-pins shining. "Hey," she calls out to them. "Is there anyone else on that flight?"

"No," says the crew member. "Oh, wait. There is one UM. She'll be out in a minute." He and the pilot hustle away.

"Do you think Mica is a UM?" Anna asks.

"I sure do hope so." Then to distract Anna Johnette adds, "What do you think UM stands for, anyway, an undulating monkey?"

Anna gets a thinking look on her face. It's like they're at home doing magnetic poetry on the refrigerator door. "A universal mosquito?"

"An unfamiliar molecule?"

"An unwanted mozzarella?"

"Good one!" says Johnette appreciatively, but the whole time she's fighting down panic. Mica isn't coming. And if she doesn't show up, what do they do next?

And then, way down where the corridor enters the terminal, someone shouts, "Anna!"

Anna throws the sign up in the air and screams, "Mica!"

"No, Anna, you're not supposed to—"

But Anna runs right by the warning that's supposed to deter non-passengers. She beelines toward a short girl dragging a suitcase with one stuck wheel.

The girl stops. Anna continues to charge. The girl doesn't look as if she expects a hug—*Don't overwhelm her,* Johnette thinks—

but Anna's a hugger. The girl drops the handle of the suitcase and the suitcase flops over. Anna throws her arms around her friend and it seems to Johnette that the girl hugs back, but she can't say for sure because just then a flight attendant strides up purpose-fully and thrusts an official-looking piece of paper at her. "Johnette Walker? I'll need a signature and a picture ID before I can release Mica to you."

"In a minute, please." Johnette doesn't want to miss this scene. The flight attendant, still holding the piece of paper, clicks a pen point in and out.

After the hug knocks the suitcase over, Anna grabs the handle and pulls it along behind her, but they only go a few feet before they stop. Anna lifts her hat and points out the spot in her hair where the scissors slipped. Mica clutches a clump of her own hair and holds it out like, see? They both laugh.

Each girl now has a hand on the suitcase handle. They walk in matched strides.

Mica says something and they stop again. They lay the suit-case down on its back. The security screener is watching them. In a minute he'll have to tell them that they need to move into the main terminal, for security reasons, but Johnette decides he must have kids of his own. He's watching the girls with a smile on his face. *Leave them alone,* she thinks. *Don't wreck this.*

The pen clicks faster and faster. "If you'll just sign this and show me some ID..." the flight attendant repeats.

By the time Johnette signs the official piece of paper and hands the woman her driver's license, the security guy has moved in on the girls—and Mica is showing him a giant seashell she pulled from her suitcase. Mica says something and his eyebrows shoot up.

Bet she just hit him with the Latin name, Johnette thinks.

At just that moment Anna looks up and sees her watching. It was hard to convince Mrs. Riley that having Mica for a month-long visit was a good idea, but the smile Anna gives her makes it all worthwhile. It's a smile that doesn't have any shadows in it. It's just pure happy.

Ignoring the Homeland Security sign herself, Johnette strides toward the girls.

Anna tugs at the sleeve of Mica's short jacket. "Hey, Mica. I want you to meet my mom, Miss Johnette. Mom, this is Mica, my sorta sister."